It's not her. It can't be, Nick thought to himself.

Yet there was something about Valerie that seemed to reach back too far to be faked. How could she possibly have learned the quirks that were Valentina's? Little things such as the half-dimple that creased her right cheek when she smiled. The way her fingers played unconsciously with the hem of her blazer when she was nervous. The way she tilted her head and looked at him with implicit trust.

And he really didn't like the way looking at her kicked up his blood.

Could Valentina have finally come home? But he had proof—the blanket, the deathbed confession of the chauffeur. There was even a guy in prison serving time for the kidnapping.

Damn her for showing up now.

And damn him for doubting what his own eyes showed him.

D0018018

SYLVIE KURTZ

PULL OF THE MOON

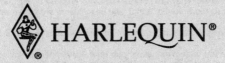

TORONTO • NEW YORK • LONDON
AMSTERDAM • PARIS • SYDNEY • HAMBURG
STOCKHOLM • ATHENS • TOKYO • MILAN • MADRID
PRAGUE • WARSAW • BUDAPEST • AUCKLAND

For Chuck—for telling me I'm wonderful no matter what.
For Ann, Joyce and Lorrie—for your continuing friendship.
I would like to extend a special thank-you to the
following people for their help: Jennifer LeDuc Cusato,
Marianne Mancusi, Denise Robbins and Jared Shurtliff.

ISBN-13: 978-0-373-22960-4
ISBN-10:   0-373-22960-7

PULL OF THE MOON

Copyright © 2006 by Sylvie Kurtz

www.eHarlequin.com

Printed in U.S.A.

ABOUT THE AUTHOR

Flying an eight-hour solo cross-country in a Piper Arrow with only the airplane's crackling radio and a large bag of M&M's for company, Sylvie Kurtz realized a pilot's life wasn't for her. The stories zooming in and out of her mind proved more entertaining than the flight itself. Not a quitter, she finished her pilot's course and earned her commercial license and instrument rating.

Since then, she has traded in her wings for a keyboard, where she lets her imagination soar to create fictional adventures that explore the power of love and the thrill of suspense. When not writing, she enjoys the outdoors with her husband and two children, quilt-making, photography and reading whatever catches her interest.

You can write to Sylvie at P.O. Box 702, Milford, NH 03055. And visit her Web site at www.sylviekurtz.com.

Books by Sylvie Kurtz

CAST OF CHARACTERS

Valerie Zea—Her assignment as a segment producer for *Florida Alive* is to find out as much as she can about the twenty-five-year-old kidnapping of Valentina Meadows Callahan.

Nicolas Galloway—Rita protected him and his mother when they needed help getting away from Nick's father. Now it's his turn to protect Rita from the pseudo-Valentinas who seek to separate Rita from her fortune.

Rita Meadows—Against all evidence, Rita believes her daughter is still alive. She'll do anything to find her—even take a chance on the kooks Nicolas works so hard to discourage.

Holly Galloway—She found the courage to leave her husband to offer her son a more stable life.

Edmund Meadows—Rita's uncle owns the TV station where Valerie works.

Gordon Archer—Nick's father is famous for his get-rich-quick schemes.

Marissa Hatch Zea—Her secret could destroy both her and Valerie's world.

Mike Murakita—Valerie's photographer isn't keen on this assignment.

Dr. Evan Gardner—This paranormal researcher is there to uncover a ghost.

Kirby Cicco—This man is serving a life sentence for Valentina's murder.

Prologue

October brought out the ghosts. Not that they weren't always there for Rita Meadows, but in October, they crowded her, pressured her, demanded she set them free.

Alone in her big bed, she couldn't sleep. Returning home to Moongate tended to do that to her, especially now that the anniversary was fast approaching. She had to readjust to the mansion, to the eerie weight of the leaden memories its wooden facade held prisoner. This was her first night home since her secret trip to Chicago—one Nicolas wouldn't approve of—and already she wished she could leave again, if only for a little while longer.

Maybe she should just skip October this year, come back in November when the ghosts' grip lost its fierceness. After all these years of vigil, her aging bones deserved a rest. She could spend October bobbing on a yacht in the Caribbean or tasting her way through Napa Valley.

Oblivion. That would be nice.

She bolted up at the renegade thought. "No, baby, I didn't mean that."

Her fault. Her cross to bear. She hadn't given up hope; she never would. But sometimes, she just wanted the pain to end.

Outside a storm boiled over Mount Monadnock and down into the valley, spilling into Moonhill. Like a brew bubbling over from a witch's pot, rain flooded against the roof and deluged the windowpanes with waterfalls. Wind pounded against the walls, and thunder reverberated through the empty halls. A tomb would feel much like this: cold, dark and empty.

The plague of insomnia had her staring at the ceiling, finding the face of evil in the plaster as a necromancer might in a scrying bowl. One answer to one question. That's all she wanted. Why was it so hard to find?

The storm's fury ebbed, and the faint whimpers of a baby's cries imprinted themselves on the air. She slid under the covers as the frightened pitch increased. Closing her eyes, fisting her hands against her ears, did nothing to vanquish the child's terror.

Only one thing would.

Tears coursing down her cheeks, she rose from her bed. As she'd done on countless other nights, she crept into the hallway and wound her way toward the third-floor tower room. There she pressed the plunger of the antique iron latch. The door creaked open and the cries instantly ceased.

The cries weren't real. They were just a trick of her mind, giving form to her guilt. There were no babies here, dead or otherwise—only her misguided hope.

Wrapping one arm around her stomach, she stepped into the yellow pool of artificial light burning from the night-light that had made Valentina feel safe. An expectant hush weighted the room as if the walls were listening for the missing four-year-old's return.

Nothing had changed in this room. For twenty-five years the tic-tac-toe play rug, the child's bed with its princess-pink canopy, the pile of stuffed animals on the butterfly-stenciled storage chest had remained as they were on the day Valentina had disappeared.

The static landscape her daughter had left behind stared back, ripe with accusation, and a lightning jag of pain, raw and deep, clawed at Rita's heart. "I'm so sorry, baby, so sorry."

If she could do it all over again… But no, there was no rewinding time.

As Rita turned to leave, a gray shape formed along her peripheral vision.

A sigh, no more than an exhale, seemed to sough against her ear. *Mama.*

Breath held, Rita stopped and pressed a hand to her thundering heart. "Valentina?"

The hope, so sharp in her voice, cut through the thick fog of memories. Of course not. What had the doctor called it? Projection? The disappointment of reality resettled heavily on her shoulders.

"No, Rita. It's me, Holly."

Rita swiveled toward the doorway where her faithful friend and housekeeper stood, her long gray braid a beacon in the night.

"I thought I heard—" Rita's hand fluttered like a surrender flag toward the window. "I thought Valentina was… home."

Holly's solid arm wrapped around Rita's waist, supporting her, and gently led her away from the center of her agony.

"You must think me a fool."

"No, of course not, Rita. It was just the storm. Let me walk you back to your room."

"I'm okay." Shoulders stooped, Rita shook off Holly's helping hands and made her way back into her bedroom alone, fading into the shadows of the house…just another ghost.

Chapter One

Pewter shrouded the October afternoon as Valerie Zea and Mike Murakita—her photog and soundman for the shoot—made their way to Moonhill, New Hampshire. Here and there a red maple leaf or a yellow beech leaf, still clinging stubbornly to a limb, flickered like a tongue of fire.

Valerie had seen photos of the White Mountains blazing with fall color, of the misty lakes like milky beads of moonstone wreathing the endless vistas from high atop the mountains, of the bellowing moose that required warnings to motorists every few miles on the highway. And she'd wanted to see all that rugged beauty, so different from the lush flatness of Central Florida she was accustomed to.

She'd been disappointed enough when she'd read that the Old Man of the Mountain—a nature-made Indian head of stacked boulders perched precariously on the side of a mountain for centuries—had fallen a few years ago and no longer watched over Franconia Notch. Just the name—Franconia Notch—conjured up a grand and magnificent picture. Not that they were anywhere near the White

Mountains, since Moonhill was located in the southern part of the state. But the fog was cheating her out of her anticipated sense-stunning experience.

She compared the MapQuest directions she'd gotten online against the road signs popping up out of the low clouds on the narrow road. "Turn here."

Mike jerked the car onto the country lane. "A little more warning next time."

"Aye, aye, captain."

On the right side, a low stone wall framed a cemetery whose granite headstones and statuary poked out of the mist. Not quite on the scale of a mountaintop view, but filled with mystery, suspense and intrigue.

On the left, a Stick-style Victorian with a wraparound porch glared through the murk like some sort of movie set haunted house. Orange fairy lights dripped from the eaves. Giant glow-in-the-dark spiders and webs clung to the decorative trusses. A life-size mummy with arms outstretched seemed poised to lumber out of the six-foot tall black coffin leaning against the oak by the front walk. On the lawn, strobes blasted on and off at intervals, lighting up red-eyed bats, moaning zombies and shrieking gargoyles. There were enough special effects there to make a Hollywood techie jealous.

"Talk about overkill," she said. The overblown drama of the scene would make an interesting segment of its own, though, especially if she could find a Florida angle to it. Maybe the owner's parents were part of the snowbirds that flocked to the Sunshine State every winter. She made a mental note to look into the possibilities before she pitched the idea to Higgins, her executive producer. He'd appreciate maximizing the bang for his travel-expense buck.

She peered at the web-encrusted mailbox by the entrance for the address. "We've got a way to go yet."

Mike warbled his voice to make it sound spooky, but it came out sounding more like the Count on *Sesame Street*. "Maybe it's the local haunted house for Halloween." He shot her a mischievous grin. At thirty, he still looked like a kid with his boyish face that couldn't grow a beard, except for a sparse tuft on his chin that looked like a smudge of dirt. "Want some B-roll of that for your segment?"

"Yeah, Higgins would go for that. He's already ticked off Krista's doctor wouldn't let her fly, and he had to send second-choice me to do the job." The assignment was high priority since it had come down as a special order from Edmund Meadows, the station's owner. He'd requested a package about the kidnapping of his great-niece twenty-five years ago in hopes of stirring up some new evidence that could lead to finding the missing girl.

"On the plus side. He put you above Bailey."

Bailey-the-Beautiful who had Higgins wrapped around her long legs. Valerie snorted. There was too much at stake for Higgins to risk needing to mop up after Bailey. "Efficiency won out over looks."

"Either that or he couldn't give her up for four whole nights."

"There is that."

High on Windemere Drive, Moongate Mansion materialized out of the shifting mist. First the six-foot granite wall and the black iron gate, canted open, daring intruders to trespass. Then the estate itself, a gray nineteenth-century Victorian with an eclectic mix of Italianate and Queen Anne. Each generation of Meadowses, seeking no doubt to stamp their mark, had added to the original two-story, four-room house until it sprawled over 13,000 square feet, looking like some sort of Frankenstein creature.

Valerie couldn't imagine living in such a dreary place, especially with its constant bruise of painful memories. But she also understood why Rita Meadows stayed. For Valentina. If she came back, her home would be there, waiting for her, lights shining bright, and her mother would be there, too, arms open wide.

Valerie swiped surreptitiously at the moistness in her eyes. Her mother called Valerie's tendency toward the melodramatic maudlin. But what could she say, she liked happy endings. There were so few of them in real life.

Mike crunched the rental up the gravel drive. She rolled the window down for a better look at the house. The scent of decomposing leaves and wood smoke infiltrated the car. Dark trees on each side of the lane swayed and whispered as if in warning. Ahead light gleamed from what seemed like a hundred windows, brightening the gloom of the day with their glow. But even that wasn't enough to dispel the aura of decay that clung to the house's wooden boards like ivy.

Her blood quickened as the voice-over wrote itself in her head. Cohost Dan Millege's deep bass vibrated with gravity in her brain, hitting just the right emotional tone for the introduction to a twenty-five-year-old kidnapping. She ripped out her portfolio and scratched furious notes to capture the inspiration before it vanished. "Can't you just feel the mystery in the air? We *have* to get the fog on tape before it lifts."

Off to the side of the house, Mike shoved the rental into Park. "Don't you ever look at anything without seeing it from a story angle?"

Valerie shrugged. The story *was* everything. She couldn't explain it to Mike—or to her mother—but some inner force drove her to ferret information, any information, about everything. Her mother called it a disease and, although Valerie preferred to label her flaw as curiosity, she couldn't quite disagree. She couldn't remember a time when she wasn't looking for something, anything, to fill the hollowness in her soul.

We give you everything, Valerie. Isn't that enough?

It should be, and that it wasn't, truly pained her.

This curiosity had landed her the job as coordinating producer for *Florida Alive*, a half-hour magazine format program that aired Monday through Friday at seven, right after the nightly news, and showcased people, places and things of interest in the state.

So, okay, *Florida Alive* was considered soft news and didn't exactly hit life-altering issues. That didn't mean she couldn't find the deeper meaning in a sand sculpture competition or the creation of pastry masterpieces or the raising of camels. What fired up other people, what gave their lives purpose, what made them feel alive fascinated her. Passion fascinated her. And traveling all over the state to see new places and meet all sorts of different people was an amazing bonus for a girl with wanderlust who hadn't traveled more than fifty miles from home until after graduating from college.

Mike peered at the massive house, no doubt gauging shot angles. "So, you think she's dead?"

Valerie's gaze climbed up the polygonal tower, and a shiver rippled down her spine. Crazy, but the child's frantic cries seemed to vibrate against Valerie's chest and the child's panic to shudder down Valerie's limbs, making her hands cold and clammy.

She reached for the French vanilla coffee she'd bought at the Dunkin' Donuts a few towns back and warmed her hands against the paper cup. With a fervor that rocked her, she wanted that baby to be safe somewhere. Who took a child from her own bedroom? Who could purposely cause such grief? And why?

Valerie swallowed and ripped her gaze back to Mike. "After twenty-five years…"

"It's kind of sad to think of this lady pining away for her dead kid for so long."

But what else could a mother do? Without proof of death, she couldn't give up. As much as Valerie and her mother didn't see eye-to-eye on practically anything, her mother would search the ends of the earth to find her, and Valerie would do the same for her mother. Recalling their argument that morning, Valerie winced and made a mental note to call once she got back to the inn and apologize. "That's why we have to do the best job we can with the story."

Mike slanted her a knowing grin. "You just want Krista's job when she goes off on maternity leave."

Valerie had eyed the news producer's job ever since Krista had announced her pregnancy. It was a stepping-stone to producing harder-hitting stories, one Valerie had to cross if she ever wanted to get to New York. "So what if I do?"

Mike cranked off the engine and shot his hands up. "Hey, I'm just saying, word is, you've got competition for the spot."

Bailey-the-Beautiful. "Sure and steady wins the race."

"Only in fables, babe."

"Don't call me babe."

Racking up a mental to-do list, Valerie juggled her cell phone, purse, portfolio of notes and cup of coffee. "I'll introduce myself to Ms. Meadows and set up a time to look through her archives tomorrow. I'll see if I can find more potential witnesses. I have that prison interview set up for Thursday. Then we can shoot Ms. Meadows's interview on Friday." Which would mean spending the whole weekend editing to get the package ready to air next week. No wonder she didn't have a social life. That wouldn't be so bad, except for the coming-home-to-only-a-dog part. "You can get started on the exteriors. Can you get a tracking shot coming up the drive? Low angle so the house seems to pop out of the fog? Maybe a Dutch angle to make it look spooky?"

"No problem."

Mike had a great eye. She could count on him getting her the shots she needed. She pointed at the third-floor room of the turret. "That's where she disappeared from.

Make sure you get some shots from all angles. And this living room window, too. That's where the party was held. I want the window to look as if it's glowing so the viewer can imagine the party in full swing."

"Got it." Mike got out of the car. "Keep it short, will ya? I haven't eaten anything all day, except for those stale airline pretzels."

Valerie nodded distractedly. She'd add festive sounds during editing for the full effect. Sipping on her coffee, she stared at the window. What was it like to realize that while you were entertaining guests someone had sneaked upstairs and stolen your only child while she slept? Her heart tripped on a beat. The guilt had to crush poor Rita Meadows.

Mike was sorting through his gear in the trunk of the rental by the time she reached the solid-oak front door. She was about to ring the antique bell when the door blew open and the hard body of a man, carrying a briefcase and an air of hurry nearly crashed into her.

"Who are you? What do you want?" The timbre of his voice was deep and vibrant, echoing in the cavern of the foyer behind him. Costumed in a thousand-dollar suit and a hundred-dollar haircut, he exuded the righteous bearing and win-at-all-costs menace of a corporate sharpshooter. At the sight of those eyes, so dark and primal, a flash of awakening skittered through her brain and a choked jolt of something more acute than simple recognition made her catch her breath.

Nicolas Galloway. The man Rita Meadows had hired to run her father's investment firm after Wallace Meadows's death.

And, wow, Nick-the-Pit-Bull certainly lived up to his reputation as a rabid guardian. Voted most eligible, yet most elusive bachelor of New England by *Boston Magazine*. Smooth, charming and appealing. And definitely effective, if his investment track record was true. Although why anyone would want to pursue a man who ran his love life like an investment was beyond her understanding.

Somewhere over Virginia, she'd decided that he was going to be a problem. Meeting him did nothing to change her mind. But she could put personal prejudices aside. She pinned on a smile, freed one hand and stuck it out. "Hi, I'm Val—"

He fired a poison eye-dart at her. "Good God, don't tell me you're one of *them*—"

"I'm—"

"How did you get past the security?"

"The gate was—"

"I don't have time for this today. Go away and don't bother coming back. We won't even talk to you unless you agree to a DNA test, and you'll need to contact our lawyer's office for that."

He tried to bulldoze his way past her, posture straight, a relentless quality on a face with an unsmiling mouth and a strong bone structure. Armored with her portfolio, purse and cup of coffee, she stepped in front of him, blocking his path. She may look small enough to squash, but he wasn't going to step all over her that easily.

Their eyes connected like lightning, and Valerie had a sense of space rushing dizzily. Wow, those eyes. Beneath the power, they bore a scar of pain. And sadness. How could that be when his bio spelled out an idyllic childhood?

Get real, Valerie. She shook her head. Figuring out what made Nicolas Galloway tick wasn't on her busy agenda.

"I'm Valerie Zea, like sea." Her name—like her life—seemed an abbreviation of something bigger. "I'm the coordinating producer for WMOD-TV in Orlando, Florida. Ms. Meadows is expecting me."

"What for?" His icy calm chilled the already cool air and made her wish she'd put on more layers under her blazer.

Stay professional. You were invited. You have the right to be here. "We're producing two segments on her daughter's kidnapping twenty-five years ago."

Without a word, he pulled her inside.

"Hey, let go of me!"

He slammed the door shut behind them. Panes in the narrow windows framing the door reverberated in their casings. Light glazed the walls of the foyer with false warmth, clouding details, reviving that dizzy feeling. For a moment, her system went haywire at the thought of being caged with him inside this house. Reaching for the closest solid thing, she steadied herself on the firm bicep of her captor, then recoiled with pinball speed at the thought of seeking safety there.

She yanked her arm to free her elbow from the hand he'd clamped around it and frowned at him when he didn't immediately let go. "I'd say a refresher course is in order."

"Pardon me?"

"Manners. Last time your style was in, men wore mammoth skins and carried clubs."

He jerked her arm down as if to plant her in place and gave a sharp growl. "Stay here and don't move."

Movements tight and controlled, he spun on his heel and headed into the bowels of the house.

"Sure thing, Mr. Galloway. I'll be right here when you come back to apologize."

NICK FOUGHT HIS TEMPER all the way to Rita's sitting room on the second floor. He hated that the mere sight of the intruder had saturated him with a sense of fullness the way food, water and air never could, just because she looked like Valentina would, and part of him was still searching for his childhood friend.

A mask. A fraud. Just another scam artist out to separate Rita from her fortune. How could his brain let itself get fooled so easily?

Valentina was dead.

The woman's pale blue eyes had met his straight and clear, dancing with eager life and a streak of stubborn resistance. She'd done her homework, all right. Hair the color of moonlight. Natural, not bottle-bought like so many others. He'd noted things about her he hadn't wanted to notice—like the gingery smell of her skin, like the crescent scar at her temple, like the heat of certainty that she belonged in this house.

He liked even less the twitch in his chest that had been much too close to panic. Just the thought of her now shocked him all over again.

Valentina. When would she stop haunting him?

And pseudo-Valentinas, would they ever stop showing up on Moongate's doorstep preying on Rita's hopes?

He hung on to his control long enough to stop and knock on Rita's door rather than barrel right through.

Rita looked up, a flush creeping over her too-pale skin, like a kid caught with her hand in the cookie jar. Her hands folded over the age-progressed image of Valentina that had arrived in that morning's mail. His heart sank. Why did she insist on torturing herself like this every October?

"Did you forget something, Nicolas?" Though still regal in bearing, she seemed to have shrunk in the past few years, as if the burden of hope was finally getting too much to bear. He wanted to ease her pain, but she wouldn't buy any of his proofs—the blood, the DNA, even the conviction.

Hand still on the brass doorknob, he squeezed it with all his might to keep his irritation out of his voice. "There's a woman downstairs who claims you're expecting her."

"From Edmund's television station?"

He nodded.

"Yes, she's the coordinating producer who'll help me air Valentina's story." Rita's spine straightened and her chin jutted out as if she were readying for a fight. That wasn't how he wanted things to stand between them.

How could Edmund Meadows have let his niece talk him into this folly? "I wish you'd talked to me."

"Why? So you could tell me I was a doddering old fool?"

"She'll hurt you. Like all the others." Nick had gotten

good at sniffing out frauds. He knew this woman's type. The kick in the gut he'd gotten when he'd seen her outside determined to get in only proved she was nothing more than another opportunist.

He jerked his chin at the photo beneath Rita's hand. She'd be embarrassed if he told her he knew about her nightly supplications with God in the tower room. But if he told her, then he'd have to admit his own guilt, and he couldn't bear the look of disappointment in her eyes. "She looks just like the picture."

Rita's gaze went wide and a little desperate. Her hands flattened over the photo, covering it completely. "She works for the station."

"This pretender's good. I'll give her that." Patient and resourceful. Hitting just the right notes to instantly win Rita's confidence. The worst kind of con artist. He should know; that same blood ran through his veins. "She could've been using her job to dig deeper into your past."

"You're reaching, Nicolas." Rita searched through the Notes section of her red leather agenda and tapped a paragraph on the page. "Valerie Zea has worked at WMOD for six-and-a-half years. She started as an intern right after college and has moved up to coordinating producer. She took a year off after her father died, but came back. Last year she won an Emmy for a segment she produced on a private investigator who specializes in missing children. Simon Higgins, the executive producer, tells me she's the best person for the job."

Was Higgins in on this farce? What would he gain by it? Time to run some background checks and stop this before the situation got out of control. "I'm trying to protect you from another fraud."

"I understand." Rita glanced at her notes. "She's requested access to the archives for research, and I've agreed to let her sort through my collection."

A growl formed at the base of Nick's throat, but he swallowed it back. "You're inviting trouble, and you hired me to keep you out of trouble."

"You do your job well, Nicolas. This time, though, you're wrong."

"Rita—"

Rita closed her agenda with a snap. "She'll want to interview you and Holly, as well."

Something in Nick froze. "No, that's not going to happen. I'm not going to put my mother through public humiliation again."

Rita's lips quivered into a tremulous smile. "It's the twenty-fifth anniversary. I have to do something. Someone knows where my baby is. I just want to bring her home."

And like that, a mountain of shame swamped him. Rita had exhausted every possible avenue to find Valentina— the police, private detectives, offering exorbitant rewards for information and promising no questions asked if only her daughter was returned. She'd followed every lead, no matter how thin. Once, on another anniversary, she'd even admitted she'd take a body just to know for sure what had happened to her precious daughter.

"Rita," he started, but had no idea what to say to ease her grief and make her see that her desperation would only add to her pain.

Her pale blue eyes turned to him. "I know you think I'm a fool, but I don't care. I know Valentina is alive." She banged her chest with a fist. "I can feel her in my heart."

How could he argue with that? Which didn't mean he had to set her free with the wolves. "Okay, but I'm not leaving you alone with her."

Rita stood, tucked her agenda against her chest, blood-red against her ice-blue blouse. "Don't you have a meeting with Emma Hanley and Carter Stokke about the Valentina Pond project?"

Another scam as far as he was concerned, but Rita's friend, Emma, had made a killing on Phase One, and Rita thought that, if she got in on Phase Two, it would add value to the acreage she owned on the back side of the pond. So he'd run the numbers for her and give her the black-and-white proof of his initial gut feeling. "It'll wait. You're more important."

She rounded her desk and squeezed him into a quick hug. "Thank you, Nicolas, for indulging me."

Stepping back, he nodded. She was no more than a small and fragile bird in his arms. "I'll go get her. We'll meet you in the library."

Nick's steps ate up the Oriental runner lining the hallway. Cripes, he didn't need this.

Loyalty to Rita as much as love for this place kept him rooted at Moongate. Though he was raised at the mansion, he didn't mistake himself for something he wasn't. And although Rita treated him like a son, he was ultra-aware he wasn't family. He was CEO of Meadows Investments. Nothing more. He understood that his value here was in his achievements. Which was why he'd worked at building an identity for himself outside the mansion walls with the soccer and the tutoring and the carpentry. Yet he was determined not to let Rita down, to prove she could count on him to watch out for her best interests—just as she'd once watched over him and his mother when they were helpless.

Mostly, he needed to prove that his will was stronger than the tainted blood that ran through his veins.

He wouldn't let anyone con Rita out of a single penny. He knew all the tricks. After all, he'd learned from a master.

No pseudo-Valentina with dreams of easy riches was going to get the best of him, no matter how realistic her mask.

Chapter Two

Valerie waited, as ordered, in the foyer. Not because she was afraid of Nicolas Galloway, even though his dark look and sharp bite were enough to intimidate anyone, but because there was no point in stirring up trouble until she absolutely needed to.

Save your spit for the important stuff, kiddo, Higgins had told her early in her career. *Learn to pick your fights.*

She was expected at Moongate. After all, Rita Meadows *had* requested the interview. She would allow Valerie to do her job.

The station could always send someone else, Valerie supposed. Bailey, for example. But there wasn't enough time. Not if the package was going to air in time for the anniversary as Ms. Meadows wanted. And in a time crunch, Valerie could get things done that would send Bailey in a tizzy.

Valerie glanced at her watch, then sipped the last cold drop of the French vanilla coffee, clinging to her otherwise empty cup, and wished for more. Her restless feet

paced the foyer, and her gaze speared into the hall, antici-
pating Nicolas Galloway's return.

The slow *bong* of a grandfather clock reverberated
from somewhere far inside and echoed in the chambers of
her head. The baneful peal shot her back to the middle of
the night when she'd woken up a prisoner in her tangled
sheets, bitter terror clinging to her skin along with the
sweat. She had an overpowering urge to rub the hairs
writhing on the back of her neck, to run.

It's just a house. And she wasn't stressed. Tired because
of the early flight, maybe, but not stressed. So there was
no reason for her to think of the dream.

But the hall boring into the dark heart of the house had
the cold breath of a mausoleum. The smell of dusty funeral
roses drifting from it plucked at her memory. "One too
many creepy black-and-white movie, Valerie."

She toyed with the empty coffee cup, looking for a
place to dispose of it. What was taking Nicolas Galloway
so long? How long did it take to say, *Hey, the person
you're expecting is here?*

Faraway giggles echoed somewhere over her shoulder.
Well, it was about time. Valerie turned toward the stairs
and the foyer shifted before her, setting off a jerky projec-
tor-like run of memories she had no right to own.

As if the outside fog had crept inside, the edges of the
room blurred. The cream paint on the walls darkened to
caramel. A cut glass vase filled with pumpkin-colored
mums appeared on the small marble-topped table. A
gilded mirror reflected the bouquet, making it pop. A red
kick ball sailed in from the open front door, bounced with

a wet *thwack* on the polished pine floor and right into the vase, knocking it to the floor. Water, broken flowers and jagged pieces of glass spread over the floor like some sort of modern art mosaic. Two sets of children's hands reached for the shards.

"It's okay. Here. Nobody'll know."

One pulled open the drawer of the decorative table and hid the broken glass inside. The other gathered the flowers.

"Shh, don't tell."

Valerie shook her head and the smoky scene vanished. The table and mirror were still there, but the bouquet and vase were gone. She looked down at her coffee cup. "Wow, that was some potent stuff."

Before she could stop herself, she stepped to the table and opened the drawer. Empty. "What, you expected to find broken glass?"

With a half laugh that rebounded against the ceiling of the foyer, she closed the drawer. She stopped midslide when the chandelier's light caught the glint of something shiny trapped in the seams.

She ran a finger along the inside edge and gasped an "Ouch" when something pricked her skin. On the tip of her index finger stood a splinter of clear glass. She drew it out and sucked on the bead of blood left behind.

Doesn't mean anything, she told herself. Could be from anything—a mirror, a lightbulb or a glass. Pocketing the bloody splinter, she willed her racing heart to slow. She left her hand balled inside the pocket of her blazer to dampen its shaking.

"Obviously, you've had too much coffee." She shouldn't have stopped for that last large cup. Bad for her nerves. Bad for her heart. Hadn't the doctor warned her just last month to cut back to stop the palpitations?

She'd probably read about the vase incident during her research and it had stuck in her mind. Wouldn't be the first time. This feeling of déjà vu happened to her more often than she liked to admit. She'd read something, see a photograph, and then, once she got on location, she'd have that feeling of having been there before.

But never this real. A tight feeling coiled in her gut.

"Get a grip." Nothing to get spooked about. One of her high school teachers had called this ability of hers to recall almost everything she'd ever seen eidetic memory and seemed fascinated by it. Of course, that was after he'd accused her of cheating on a test, and she'd had to prove to him that everything on the page had come straight from her brain and not Mark Peach's paper.

Spinning away from the scene of the mirage, she forced herself to concentrate on the collection of Currier & Ives prints, showing off the same scene of a country lane and pond in four seasons. The house in the background looked remarkably like Moongate Mansion. Maybe she could use them as a montage to show the passage of time.

"That's better." Work was her salvation. When it came to work, her fate was in her hands, not in some monster's from a dream. She could do this. She'd done it hundreds of times before. The only pressure on her was the one she was putting on herself. "Stick to the plan."

Houses, according to a psychologist she'd once interviewed for a segment on dream analysis, were a metaphor for the human psyche. This one seemed rusted in time. Haunted almost, like a restless mind. Maybe that's what Rita wanted by looking back into the past—a cure. If she understood what had happened to Valentina, then she could let go of her child and finally find peace.

The floor of the hall thundered, and Nicolas Galloway reappeared, long, determined strides making short work of the distance between them.

"About time," she mumbled, tugging her blazer back in place with her free hand.

His expression remained frozen in the feral position, and instead of an apology, he barked, "Follow me."

Sheesh, he didn't even pause to see if she followed, just assumed she would. She was used to following directions, but unbending commands were another thing. And she'd had just about enough of going through an intermediary to get to her appointment. "I really need to speak with Ms. Meadows."

"You're in luck. You're getting your wish."

As she scrambled after Nick, the raspberry brambles on the hall wallpaper shifted as if rustled by a breeze. The smell of burned toast stung her nose. The scraping of a knife against dry bread scratched at her brain.

"It'll be just fine. See?" A woman's voice. *"Now, which do you want, strawberry or blueberry preserve?"*

Valerie stopped and peered into the dining room, set with Lenox china, Pairpoint crystal and silver-plated dinnerware.

"What are you doing?"

At the boom of Nick's voice, the image vanished, leaving behind an empty table and chairs. Valerie swiveled her head to look at Nick frowning at her from the library entrance. At least this time she remembered where the flash of memory had come from—the photograph from *Victorian Homes* of a Thanksgiving dinner at Moongate the year before Valentina disappeared. "I thought I smelled toast burning."

"Someone's bringing tea." He disappeared into the room.

Valerie hurried to catch up with him. Tea was good. Tea meant Rita Meadows would let her see the archives. Tea meant that Nicolas Galloway owed her an apology—not that she was holding her breath for one. And maybe it also meant food. Which made her think of Mike. He was going to be royally cranky that she was taking so long. A well-fed Mike was a happy Mike, and a happy Mike got her good footage. Payback from Mike, on the other hand, was never a good thing.

"Sit," Nick ordered.

Arguing right now would be a waste of breath, so she chose a wing chair that gave her width and height, and deposited her portfolio and purse on the floor at her feet and the empty coffee cup on the side table. She didn't play games, but she didn't make easy prey, either.

Nick paced the marble hearth of the fireplace as if he was drawing up some sort of war plan, and she pulled back her shoulders readying her defenses.

"We need to set some ground rules," he said. "One, you are not to wander unaccompanied on the grounds or in the house at any time. That goes for your friend with the camera outside, too. I've already sent someone to detain him."

Detain Mike? Good luck to anyone who tried to

separate Mike from his camera. "Ms. Meadows has already given her permission to shoot."

"This is nevertheless Ms. Meadows's private home and intrusion into her privacy will not be tolerated. We do not want a tabloid exposé that will exploit Ms. Meadows's pain at the tragedy of her daughter's kidnapping."

What bug had crawled up his butt? "Look, you've made it clear you don't want me here, but if you think you can intimidate me into leaving, you're wrong."

He rounded on her with *High Noon* intensity. "Right now, I'm cooperating, but don't cross me, or you'll regret the day you showed up on our doorstep."

Jeez, Louise, what did he think she was going to do? Blow her career by ticking off the man who paid her salary? "An exposé is certainly not our intention. At his niece's request, Mr. Meadows asked his executive producer to put together these segments on Valentina's kidnapping. Mr. Meadows expects clean and true reporting any time his station airs a package. This will be no exception."

"Ms. Meadows is the constant target of people who would prey on her pain for gain. There are certain facts we would rather not make public in order to protect the family from scam artists."

Okay, she could see why he might be a tad touchy on the subject. Her task was to mollify him and wow him with her ability to present a fair and balanced portrait of the family's misfortune. "I understand your point, Mr. Galloway. As I said, we're not out to prey on Ms. Meadows. But *she* was the one who asked that we tell her daughter's story with the hopes of bringing her home."

"It's been twenty-five years." The statement sounded remarkably like a trick question.

"I understand. But finding the child's…location would allow Ms. Meadows closure, don't you think?"

His presence was an iceberg in a room too small to contain him, and she was uncomfortably aware of his proximity, of his stark and grim gaze—of his pain. Then, like the incidents in the foyer and the dining room, for a flash, his face wavered. A play of light and shadows had her chest heaving with a sweet ache of longing and her arms yearning to loop themselves around his neck.

A chill pierced her skin, raised a crop of goose bumps. Her fingers clawed around the arms of the chair to keep herself from slipping into the unwanted fog once again. Her breath hitched in her throat and a pang of loss nearly swallowed her. How could that be? She shook her head and, when her gaze reconnected with his, the same unyielding glower glared back at her.

Nicolas Galloway was no friend.

Yet his eyes stirred dark echoes of her recurring dream and spiked her blood with unease. Why?

"Are you okay?" he asked, frowning.

"Too much coffee." She flashed him a smile that, to her horror, wobbled.

With a sudden jolt as if she'd hit him, he turned his back on her and resumed his pacing. "Two, we'll need approval over the final product."

Valerie shot to her feet. With the amount of blood, sweat and tears she spilled to write, shoot and edit a package, there was no way she was going to let him mess with her baby. "It doesn't work that way."

"We have to be sure you haven't inadvertently leaked privileged information."

She had the station owner and the interview subject on her side. Why was she letting him get under her skin? She forced a smile. "Well, then, you'll have to take that up with the executive producer. Keep in mind that I do have a tight production schedule to adhere to if Ms. Meadows's story is to air in time for the kidnapping's anniversary."

Wrong tactic, of course. She knew that the second she uttered the words. Keeping the package off the air was exactly what Nicolas Galloway wanted.

"That, of course, is your problem." Nick's pacing came to an abrupt halt and his gaze fixed on the doorway.

Rita Meadows paused at the entrance to the door, holding on to the door frame as if she were dizzy. There was a lot of that going on today. Someone needed to check the furnace and see if the carbon monoxide level was okay.

Rita's recovery was quick. She pasted a work-the-room smile on her sculpted face, extended a hand and welcomed Valerie with the practiced ease of someone used to dealing with people. "You must be Valerie. Mr. Higgins speaks highly of you."

"As he does of you." Rita's hand was cold and brittle in Valerie's and a wave of sympathy made Valerie squeeze warmth into her grip.

Close-up, even with her understated makeup, Rita

looked hollow-eyed, a little too thin, a little too pale. Her hair, the color of expensive champagne, was twisted elegantly at her nape, giving her a fragile kind of beauty that seemed somehow tragic to Valerie.

Nick rushed to Rita's side, cupped her elbow and led her to the sofa, where he stood beside her on guard like the pit bull of his reputation. *Stray out of line, get too personal,* his cutting expression said, *and I'll rip you to shreds.*

Aye, aye. Message received, she telegraphed back, and his frown deepened.

She could see why some women might fall for him. The primitive quality he exuded told a woman that, as long as he was there, she would be safe from predators. For many— her friend Sheree among them—that promise of savage protection was the fodder of dreams. Personally, Valerie already had too much overprotection in her life. The last thing she needed was to add a man's shadow to the one already stalking her.

Rita looked up at Nick, touched his arm. "Is Holly bringing tea?"

Nick gave a sharp nod, but his quick eye shift toward the door betrayed his uncertainty. He wasn't going to leave to check on tea when there was an intruder sitting in his employer's library waiting to pounce on her.

Chill, she wanted to say. *I don't bite.*

"I know you must be tired from the flight," Rita said to Valerie, "so I won't keep you long."

"I just wanted to introduce myself and set up a convenient time to go over your archives. I have another interview on Thursday, but I'd like to tape yours on Friday."

"You may come by to look at the archives at any time."

"Eleven." The sharpness of Nick's voice coated the air with rime. "It's the only time I have available."

"I'll be here, Nicolas," Rita said. "I can walk her through my collection."

His jaw tightened and antagonism bristled from him, but he didn't say a thing. What was it costing him to keep silent? She was starting to understand just how much Rita Meadows meant to him, how far he'd go to protect her. How could Valerie reassure this many-times-bitten pit bull she meant no harm?

"Eleven will be fine." Valerie injected light and air into her voice. "My photographer will also need access to Valentina's room and the living room, as well as the grounds."

"Yes, of course," Rita said.

"We'll keep our visit as short as possible."

"Take all the time you need. I want Valentina's story retold in all its details. You never know what will trigger someone's memory."

As Rita explained what she wanted to accomplish by airing Valentina's story, Nick stared at Valerie until the room was sucked dry of air and her head grew light.

"Nick! Nick! Watch me!" A splash of water.

"I have better things to do than watch a baby play."

"I'm not a baby."

"Are, too."

"Well, forget it, then. I'm not telling you my secret."

A lakeside gazebo with green-and-white striped awnings. Green water. Green trees. Eye-hurting blue sky. Valerie remembered seeing a picture of Nick and Valentina sipping lemonade at Rita's feet on a dock. Why was that picture coming back to her now?

"May I ask you a personal question?" Rita asked Valerie, changing subjects.

"Sure."

"How old are you?"

"I'll be thirty next May." By then she'd planned on being in New York, working as a producer for a major network in the news division—at least according to the life plan she'd drawn up when she was eighteen. Come to think of it, she'd only checked one item off that long list. "That probably sounds as if I don't have much experience—"

"Oh, no, dear, I don't doubt your qualifications. How tall are you?"

Wow, where was this coming from? And what did it have to do with her ability to shoot an interview? "Five-four." With three-inch heels. "My mother's short. That's where I get it. The shortness, I mean." Oh, good, now she was babbling. Definitely time to get solid food in her.

Rita's face crumpled. Her body curled into itself and spasmed in time to a coughing fit. The red agenda she clutched in her lap fell to the ground, spilling its contents. A photograph fluttered and landed upside down at Valerie's feet.

"Rita?" Moving with speed and athletic grace, Nick knelt at his employer's side, a glass of water in hand. "Here."

Rita sipped the water Nick offered her, but the coughing only worsened. Nick gently stood her up.

Not knowing what to do to help Rita, Valerie picked up the agenda and put the pages back in place.

"Stay here," Nick ordered, glaring at her, then escorted Rita out of the library.

Valerie picked up the photograph, turned it over and gasped. The hairstyle was wrong, and the smile was too stiff, but otherwise, the picture could be hers. "What in the world?"

Why did Rita have her picture? And why didn't she remember posing for it? What kind of twilight zone had she walked into?

After ten minutes of waiting for Nick's return, questions running laps in her mind as she studied the photograph from Rita's agenda, the coffee Valerie had had on the car ride up was putting pressure on her bladder. The tinkling of water in the brass tranquility fountain on an accent table didn't help.

A middle-aged woman entered the library, looking more like a shadow than a person with her black dress, gray hair and pale skin. Did no one in this house believe in the health benefits of a touch of sun? She carried a silver tray of tea and shortbread cookies—no toast, Valerie noted—and studied the unwelcome guest with decided wariness.

The woman clucked, her dark-brown eyes troubled. Her voice, when she spoke, was soft, but unfriendly. "Ms. Meadows will be down shortly."

"She was coughing." Valerie stuck the photograph behind her back. "Mr. Galloway took her up to her room."

"Oh, no." The woman's silver braid snaked over her shoulder as she slapped the tray onto the coffee table and hurried away, her feet making no noise on the rose-adorned carpet.

"Is there a bathroom nearby?" Valerie called after her.

The woman waved a hand vaguely to her right. "Around the corner." The woman stopped her flight. Her small hand clutched the door frame as if her nails were fangs. Closet vampire? "It'd be best if you left now."

"I want to be sure Ms. Meadows is okay."

"No good will come of you digging up bones."

"We're taping the segments at Ms. Meadows's request." Valerie was starting to feel like a broken record.

"Your act," the woman warned, shaking her head. "It won't wash. Nick'll see right through it." She turned and vanished into the dark hall.

"Good to know I'm so wanted." What was going on here? Had Higgins set her up for failure so he would have a good reason to promote Bailey over her? Something wasn't right. Not just with the room, but with the whole house.

She glanced around the library with its floor-to-ceiling stacks, its comfy chairs and cozy fireplace. Nothing about the elegant decor triggered her unwarranted fear, but she couldn't help the chill crawling up her spine.

Maybe she should leave and come back in the morning when everybody had calmed down and she'd had some food.

First, though, she had to find a bathroom.

Valerie slipped the photograph into her portfolio. She wanted to study it further, see if she could remember when it was taken. She stepped into the hall. At least this time the walls didn't ripple. The first door she tried opened into a laundry room that smelled like summer rain. The next door opened into a dark room that looked like a closet, but smelled of rose potpourri and water. Valerie fumbled for a switch and found one in the hallway. Ah, finally, a bathroom.

She relieved herself and admired the painted mural that made it seem as if she were in some enchanted garden— a watercolor background of mossy-green with pink roses, golden grasses and birds. A single blue butterfly hovered on one side of the mirror as if it were going to drink a sip of water from the sink while she washed her hands. She'd always liked butterflies, especially blue ones. As she reached to touch the gossamer wings, the lights went out, leaving her swallowed by darkness.

She sucked in a breath and wrapped her hands around the cold marble of the sink to anchor herself in the pitch-black space. Blinking madly, she tried to orient herself. A power failure? It happened a lot in old houses, didn't it?

Tamping back her irrational fear of small, dark places, she forced her frozen fingers to let go of the sink. She turned with small baby steps to keep her balance, then groped blindly for the door.

Out of the darkness, a slice of light materialized and crept into the gap between the floor and the bottom of the door. She frowned. The power was still on in the rest of the house?

A board creaked outside. She froze. "Hello?" Is anybody out there?"

She stared at the paring of light, but no shadow rippled across its path.

"Just an old house settling into its bones," she told herself, but the shaky sound of her voice didn't reassure her. *Open the door and get out of here.*

Her trembling fingers bumped against the hard wood of the door. With her heart pounding an SOS against her ribs, she patted the smooth oak until she found the knob. Her damp palms slipped on the glass knob. It wouldn't budge.

She tried again, pulling and twisting. A kind of desperate madness swept over her. "Hey! Turn on the lights! Open the door!"

She panted as she tried to control the sense of impending doom sweeping over her. The burn of tears stung her eyes and, hanging on to the knob as a child would, the craziest need to call "Mama" bubbled on her trembling lips.

Not that her mother was the kind who'd fussed over emotional outbursts. *You don't need a night-light, Valerie. You're a big girl, and big girls don't cry.*

Valerie blinked madly, survival instinct kicking back in. She banged on the door with the flat of her hand. "This isn't funny!"

Nicolas Galloway. He'd done this. Did he really think locking her in the bathroom was going to send her crying home? It would take a lot more than that to make her go crawling back to the station empty-handed.

Her grip tightened on the doorknob, and she pushed, turned and tugged with all her might. When she got out of there, she was going to strangle him. "Open the door!"

Chapter Three

Teeth bared, Valerie jammed her shoulder into the bathroom door and grunted. She'd barely connected with the wood when the door burst open, and she tumbled into Nick's arms.

His hands held her forearms in a vise-tight grip to keep her from colliding with his chest. Even through the wool blend of her blazer sleeves, the vibrating heat of his anger burned her.

"What on earth are you doing?" he asked.

"The door was stuck." She spied the wooden doorstop in his hand. This little thing was what had caused her full-blown panic attack? She snatched the offending piece of wood from his hand and held it up. "It's going to take a lot more than locking me in the bathroom to discourage me."

Even if his cheap bathroom trick had worked at scaring her—momentarily—it wasn't going to make her disappear.

Guarded tension stretched his features taut. He pushed her away, breaking the heated hum of contact where his hard fingers had dug into her forearms. "Trust me, Val, if I choose to intimidate you, you'll know."

"Valerie." She rubbed her arms against the sudden need to bury herself deeper into his embrace and breathe in the alluring scent of citrus and sandalwood of his aftershave. How crazy was that? One little scare, and like a two-year-old, she was ready to seek solace in the first pair of arms that turned up.

"So if you didn't lock me in the bathroom, who did?" The woman with the braid? These people's overprotectiveness of Rita Meadows made Valerie's mother's watchful smothering seem like neglect in comparison. "How many people work here?"

"That's none of your concern. *Val.*"

"Valerie," she insisted, narrowing her eyes at him. Had someone bribed the staff in the past? Was that where his wariness was coming from? "And it does concern me when someone locks me in the bathroom. What if you hadn't come by?"

"You made enough racket. Someone would've heard you eventually."

"That's not the point—"

"I'll handle the matter."

She stuffed the doorstop in the kerchief pocket of his suit and gave it a pat. "Fine. See that it doesn't happen again." She didn't really have a choice other than to let him "handle the matter." She wasn't here to investigate the staff's juvenile intimidation tactics. She was here to conduct interviews. "How is Ms. Meadows?"

His eyes softened for a second. "Just a cold. She'll be fine."

But something in his expression told her he was more

worried than a simple cold would warrant. "I'll come back tomorrow, then. When she's feeling better."

"That would be best."

Valerie buttoned her blazer, adding an extra buffer between them. "The photograph? From the agenda? Why does Ms. Meadows have it?"

A muscle in his jaw jumped. "It's an age progression. She has one done every year on Valentina's birthday."

Valerie's heart went out to Rita. Had she had the photo done as a way to watch her baby grow? No, Valerie decided. So she'd know what Valentina would look like if she saw her on the street somewhere. Maybe airing the segment would provide Rita with the resolution she needed.

"It, uh, looks like me." The resemblance was uncanny and the memory of that likeness sent a shiver prickling over her scalp. Had Rita thought that Valerie was her daughter? Was that why she'd asked the personal questions? Although what height had to do with anything was a puzzle.

Nick's gaze hardened and bored into her with a warning that seemed to aim straight at her heart. His voice rode a flat line that reverberated with threat. "But it isn't you, Val. Something you'd best remember. Valentina is dead. I have proof. There won't be a fat payday. Not if I can help it."

Her eyes widened and her mouth dropped open. "Is that why you're being such a jerk? You think I think I'm Valentina? That's ridiculous."

"What'll it take to make you disappear?"

"What?"

He whipped out a checkbook from the inside breast pocket of his suit jacket. "How much?"

One hand covered her heart. "You can't be serious. You think I want money?"

He stepped closer until his breath was a warm flutter against her lips. "That's all they want in the end."

Her mind was blurring again. *No, Nick, no. You know that's not true.* "They?"

"All the other girls over the years who've come knocking at the door pretending they're the long-lost Valentina." He lifted a strand of her hair, rolled it between his fingers, then tucked it behind her ear. She leaned into his hand as if she'd done this very thing before. As if he had. Jeez, Louise, she really needed some food before she went totally over the edge.

His thumb skimmed the outline of her cheek in a way that let her know that he could kill her just as easily as kiss her. Wow, where had that come from? As if she'd ever want a kiss from someone who thought she was using her job to extort money.

"I'm not like all those girls. I'm not like anyone you've ever met." She swallowed, her mouth suddenly dry. She searched the hard planes of Nick's face, looking for... what? An explanation as to why she thought he would know her? Even stranger, that she should know him? That if she could just squeeze the right place on his waist, he would double over in helpless laughter?

He flattened a hand on the door frame beside her face, caging her against the wall. "That's where you're wrong. I've met a hundred girls like you. They've all convinced themselves they're the one."

A restless menace lurked right beneath the suit. But as

much as he growled and barked and bared his teeth, he would never hurt her. The truth of that knowledge resonated soul deep. Which didn't mean she wanted to test that theory quite yet.

She planted a palm against his chest and pushed him away. "I have a mother and a good life in Florida. I don't need to borrow anybody else's. So chill, okay? You said Valentina was dead. That you had proof? What kind?"

"That's really none of your concern."

"Well, see, that's where I don't agree. Everything that concerns Valentina concerns me."

"And you think I'm just going to hand you ammunition?"

She tipped her head and squinted at him. "To fleece Ms. Meadows? No. To help me put on the best segment I can? Yes. If you have proof that Valentina is dead, then it means I need to take a different angle with the interviews."

He refused to yield. "Knowing Valentina is dead doesn't stop the crazies from showing up for a handout. The body was never found. Until it is, they prey on Ms. Meadows's hopes."

She sighed. "I can see your point, but what if she isn't dead?" As if drawn by a black hole, all she could do was look deep into the impenetrable dark brown of his eyes. *Let me in, Nick. Let me see.* That he was shutting her out hurt in a way that was beyond crazy. So was the compelling childish urge to pat his cheek and tell him that everything was going to be okay. "What if she is alive?"

"She isn't." End of conversation, his tone said. But something flickered in his eyes, leaving her with the impression he was lying. Or at least not telling her the whole truth.

A door slammed somewhere down the hall, startling Valerie out of her strange connection with Nick. Never before had she been so aware of someone. The give-and-take of his breath. The galloping pulse of blood at his neck. The prickly hint of beard along his tense jawline. And that sadness, that heavy sadness that was eating at his soul and made her want to cry.

"It's time for you to leave now." Nick straightened, yawning a canyon of space between them, and Valerie ran her hands over her arms to keep warm.

Heavy boots tromped on the floor, heading their way. A stout man with a white lion's mane poking out from a well-worn khaki fishing hat stepped into the hall. He jabbed a thumb over his shoulder. "Took me a while, but I've got the gentleman under control like you asked. He's in the car with the doors locked." He grinned, showing off square, white teeth. "Chomp is watching over him. He won't go anywhere he ain't supposed to go."

"Thanks, Lionel."

"My pleasure." Lionel doffed his fishing hat and swept it in front of him, showing Valerie the way to the front door. "I'll escort you out now, ma'am. Chomp, he don't take too kindly to strangers."

She pointed toward the library. "My things."

Nick nodded his permission, and she held her breath until she reached the library. She shook her head as if the simple gesture could release her from the grip of Nick's presence still clinging to her skin. The way he'd short-circuited her usually ordered thinking wasn't normal. Especially when it came to work.

You only have to deal with him for a couple of days, Valerie. And she'd be too busy with all the details; she'd forget he was even around.

She slipped Valentina's photograph out of her portfolio, took one last look at the woman who could be her twin and tucked it back into Rita's agenda. As sick as she was, Rita would need the comfort of her daughter's picture. "Definitely spooky, though."

But Valerie Grace Zea was born on May 13, not October 31. She was six months older than Valentina. She owned a baby album filled with pictures that featured Marissa and Ludlow Zea cradling her in the home where she'd spent all of her life, until four years ago when she'd bought her own little shoe box of a house just a mile from her parents'.

Her memory was crowded with snapshots of her life in Florida. No mansion. No fog-shrouded landscape. No Rita Meadows.

A creak made her look up and sweep the room with a glance.

Nothing there to warrant the itch between her shoulder blades, but she couldn't help trying to roll away the feeling of being watched. Portfolio clutched to her chest, she hurried back into the hall where Nick's long shadow loomed, waiting for her.

"I'll see you tomorrow, then." She adjusted her purse over her shoulder and yearned for a cup of coffee. "To look through the archives."

"Eleven."

"Eleven it is." She slanted her head and gave him her most serious look. "I'll do a good job."

His mouth flattened. "Valentina needs to be buried, not revived."

"To bury her, you have to find her. Someone out there knows where she is, and airing those segments could bring you the information you need for closure."

"Don't you think that if anyone knew where she was, they'd have said something by now? Claiming the one-million-dollar reward is much easier than pretending to be a dead child all grown-up."

"So we're back to that, huh?" Actions spoke more clearly than words. In the end, he'd see she was true to her word.

His voice, low and rough, rumbled with warning. "Secrets are called that for a reason, Val. And sometimes people want to keep their secrets buried."

Oh, yeah? What's yours? "I'm not her. But I'm not one of your pretenders, either. I'm just a woman trying to do her job." Why was it so important that he believe her?

A terrifying flicker of a smile sprang to his lips. "Make sure that's all you do."

NICK STOOD TO ONE SIDE of the window, surveying the scene below him. Valerie walked with both a dancer's grace and a sprinter's efficiency. Although she couldn't see him standing in the shadows of the third-floor tower room, she paused before entering the car and looked up. Not at Lionel and the barely controlled Doberman the caretaker held by the studded collar on the doorstep. But at him. Their gazes met across the barrier of glass and shadows, and she seemed to shiver before she disappeared into the safety of the car.

Good. She should be afraid. Fear would keep her from following through on her plan to blind Rita with her likeness to Valentina.

He wouldn't be as easy to fool.

He'd already paid a hefty price for his mistake. He picked up the floppy-eared dog that had been Valentina's favorite and buried his nose in the fur that had long ago lost its little-girl smell. In its place came the remembered sweet-and-spicy ginger scent Valerie wore. He hurled the dog back to the storage chest and scraped a hand over his face. His weakness had cost him his best friend and the only person who'd understood him.

Protecting Rita, protecting Valentina's memory were the most important things in his life. A man had to take care of his own.

He followed the track of the car down the driveway until the fog devoured it. This woman was good. Better than the rest, judging by the instant connection she'd made with Rita.

It's her, Nicolas. I can feel it. Rita's words echoed in his empty soul. She'd been ready to open her arms, her home and her heart to the charlatan. *That's why she didn't come before. She doesn't know.*

He couldn't bear the toll the inevitable pain would cost Rita. *It's not her, Rita. It can't be.*

His gaze zoomed in on the golden pine of the floor, and that horrible night sucked him back into its darkness. Rita had had the floor sanded and refinished, but Nick could still see the dark stain spreading.

The blood, he'd never stop seeing all that blood.

Or her eyes. Those half-closed, dead eyes.

His fault that she was gone.

Yet there was something about Valerie that seemed to reach back too far to be faked. His chin dropped to his chest and his eyes closed. How could she possibly have learned the quirks that were Valentina's? Little things like the half dimple that creased her right cheek when she smiled. The way her fingers played unconsciously with the hem of her blazer when she was nervous. How many sweaters had Valentina unraveled with that nasty habit? The way she tilted her head and looked at him with implicit trust. He'd never been able to scare Valentina, except with ghost stories, and then she'd looped her arms around his neck, pressed her cheek against his. *Are they gone, Nick? Are the ghosts gone?*

And he really didn't like the way looking at her kicked up his blood.

Could Rita be right? Could Valentina have finally come home? Or was Valerie pulling the ultimate con by pretending she wasn't Valentina, but seeding all the right clues?

No, Valentina was dead. He had proof—the DNA, the blanket, the deathbed confession of Rita's former chauffeur. For crying out loud, there was even a guy in prison, serving time for the kidnapping.

And the blood. All that blood.

He rubbed his eyes to blot out the sight.

Damn Valerie for showing up.

And damn him for doubting what his own eyes showed him.

Nick stalked away from the window and marched to Rita's office. He ripped the phone from the cradle and dialed the P.I. he had on retainer.

Joe Aveni might as well have called himself Joe Average. Brown hair, brown eyes in an unmemorable face. Under the layer of fat he cultivated, he hid hard muscles he exercised five days a week. He dressed forgettably and appeared no threat to either males or females. All of which rendered him incredibly efficient at cajoling information from even the most unwilling of sources. No would-be Valentina had ever been able to stand up to his scrutiny.

"I need a background check," Nick said when Joe answered.

"Hey, man, I'm backed up. It'll take me a couple of days to get to it."

"I'll double your rate."

"Ah, shoot, Nick, don't tell me you got another Valentina."

"The twenty-fifth anniversary is going to bring out all the crazies."

"Give me what you've got."

Nick gave the information he'd found on Valerie in the agenda he'd brought up from the library along with the empty take-out coffee cup.

"I'll have a quick-and-dirty for you by the end of the day," Joe said.

"Sooner."

"You realize it's already past three, don't you?"

Nick swallowed a growl. "Soonest you can."

"How deep do you want me to go?"

Nick sought the age-progressed picture from the back of Rita's agenda. Valerie's face superimposed itself on Valentina's dead eyes and stiff smile in a way he didn't like. Alive, so alive. Her blond hair rippling with light, her eyes blue beams of determination, her teasing mouth taunting him in a too-familiar way. He squeezed the tension at the back of his neck and willed the mirage to disappear. "I want to know everything about her from the first breath she ever took to what she had for breakfast this morning."

Joe cleared his throat. "Going that deep'll mean travel and a couple of days' delay. Maybe a week, depending on what turns up."

"Bill me."

The *click-click* of Joe's pen pecked at Nick's eardrum. "Can I ask what's different about this one?"

What about Valerie had made him fall for the illusion in a way none of the other frauds had?

The con, he realized. Too slick. Too choreographed. "She's too good."

Joe bellowed out a laugh. "I've got to meet this woman who has Nicolas Galloway all tied up in knots."

Nick had known only one person who could slide so smoothly through a lie and make anyone believe it was the truth. He still bore the scars of that misplaced trust, and he wasn't going to let anyone add to them.

Was he back? Because of the anniversary?

A deep, disturbing gush of anger spewed up and shook Nick to the core.

"What you have to do is get me the ammunition I need to stop her cold." Nick picked up the empty take-out cup that, even through the brown paper bag, still smelled faintly of vanilla and coffee. "Can your DNA guy extract what he needs from a cup of take-out coffee?"

"I'll find out."

"And while you're at it, I'll need a financial on Simon Higgins. He's the executive producer at WMOD-TV in Orlando." Nick took a deep breath. "And find me Gordon Archer's current whereabouts."

What Nick needed was facts. Basic, logical, hard facts. With those he could fight them all—Archer, Higgins and Valerie. Especially Valerie.

She'd come back in the morning. And he'd have to be ready for her.

AT THE OTHER END of the phone, the woman burst into tears. "Valerie's gone." Was there no end to the river she could cry? "I tried everything, but she still went."

He slapped a stack of reports into his briefcase. "I'll take care of it."

A nervous tick of nails clicked against the phone. "You won't hurt her, will you?"

He rolled his eyes toward the ceiling and shook his head. "What do you take me for?"

After all he'd done for her, the least she could do is show him a little respect and gratitude. He wasn't an idiot. Why would he want to bring attention to a mistake when he was so close to payback?

"I'm sorry." She sniffed. "I didn't mean…"

"Of course you didn't." He softened his voice. "Trust me. I'll take care of everything."

She swallowed a large bubble of air.

"Everything's fine," he insisted.

"But what if—"

"She's just doing her job."

"But…" She sighed. "Okay, if you're sure."

"I'm sure." He hung up, snatched the brochure from the desk and sneered at the mansion used as a logo. They'd airbrushed out the weeds and the neglect, but they couldn't quite hide the self-important haughtiness. He pitched the brochure into his briefcase, snapped it shut and locked it.

Valerie was at Moongate.

He reached for the custom-tailored suit jacket on his bed. She'd been warned. If she couldn't take a hint, if she got in his way, she'd have to suffer the consequences.

Then a zing of new possibility burst in his chest. He smiled as he adjusted his tie in the mirror. On the other hand, if he couldn't keep her away, maybe he could use her to his advantage.

He'd get his chance. He'd always known it would come.

Briefcase in hand, he hummed as he left the room. This time, he'd get it right. This time, no one would mistake him for shoe scum—least of all the high-and-mighty Rita Meadows.

Chapter Four

When Valerie arrived at Moongate the next morning, she'd expected to give Rita Meadows a quick greeting, then get down to the archives while Mike taped his interior shots. But plans had a way of twisting themselves around, especially when time was at a premium. Really, if a shoot ever ran smoothly, she'd think the end of the world had arrived.

She stifled a sigh. One out of two was better than none. At least Mike was on his way up to the tower room escorted by the burly Lionel.

A whippet-thin and rumpled man sat with Rita in the library. The only plus side Valerie could see to the delay was that Nick seemed even less happy to see the new arrival than he'd been at seeing her.

Nick wore a charcoal suit today, and with his crisp white shirt and power-red tie, he presented the perfect picture of the successful businessman. His protective stance at Rita's side left no doubt that, should anyone try to harm her, they would suffer his wrath.

Then there were those eyes, guarded and restrained. But an undeniable frisson of something passed between

Valerie and him when their gazes connected, and she couldn't help the hint of a smile that twitched her lips or the bubbly desire to play that infiltrated her limbs.

Do not even go there, Valerie. Nick wasn't part of the job and was way too complex for her to deal with in three days.

"Valerie! I'm so glad you're finally here." Rita's smile beamed. A strong red painted her cheeks, as if she'd gone too heavy with the blush. Her eyes had a feverish gleam to them that made Valerie think Rita should still be in bed. "There's someone I want you to meet." She patted her hand on the sofa next to her, inviting Valerie to sit.

Valerie's gaze jumped to Nick, who simply scowled at her with his cool, dark eyes. She perched a polite distance from her hostess—as far away from Nick as she could, grateful the sofa's cream fleur-de-lis back offered a barrier between them—and clipped on a smile. She'd wasted way too much of her night thinking about Nicolas Galloway to allow him to get to her today.

"This is Dr. Evan Gardner," Rita said. "He's come to work a little project for me."

Up close, Evan Gardner was shades of tan from his straight dirty-blond hair to his camel tweed jacket and scuffed boots. His forty-something face had a houndish sag to it that seemed oddly familiar.

Valerie nodded a greeting, remembering where she'd met the man before. "Nice to meet you again, Dr. Gardner."

The man might look like a fashion disaster, but he knew his stuff. She twirled her cup of take-out coffee in her hands. How long would she have to sit here before she could excuse herself to search the archives?

Nick stiffened. "You've met?"

Another layer of wariness clanked into place in Nick's eyes. Going through life suspecting everyone of having ulterior motives was a tough way to exist. Did he ever untie his starched collar? Did he ever have fun?

"At a psychic fair last year in Orlando." Valerie still got a shiver thinking about the spread of dark and gloomy tarot cards she received as part of the segment.

"Oh, that's right." Evan slapped a big hand on the thigh of his tan trousers and offered her a shaggy smile. "You interviewed me about paranormal investigation techniques."

"I never knew there were so many electronic gadgets!" Valerie turned to Rita. "Do you have a ghost in the house?"

"That's what I mean to find out." Rita poured tea and offered Valerie a cup. Although she'd rather have her coffee, and although she'd rather just get on with the job, she accepted, aware of Nick's gaze burning a disapproving hole right through her. "I met Evan in Chicago—"

"Chicago?" Nick frowned. "When were you in Chicago? Why didn't I know about this?"

A flush crept up Rita's neck. "I've been looking for someone reputable, someone you would have to listen to. So when I heard that Evan was going to be presenting a seminar at a paranormal convention in Chicago, I had to go."

"At a what?"

Rita's spoon stilled against the side of her cup. "You heard me, Nicolas. Why do you think I didn't tell you?"

"You're making me sound like the bad guy here."

Rita raised an eyebrow as if to say, "If the shoe fits," and sipped. "Evan has science behind him."

Nick planted both hands on the back of the sofa and, though his voice was controlled, Valerie sensed an inner storm blustering in him. "Hiding behind science doesn't mean he's not a quack."

Evan's gaze ping-ponged between Nick and Rita. "Uh, should I leave?"

"No," Rita insisted. "Evan is a professional ghost hunter with scientific credentials, Nicolas. He majored in history and archeology, which taught him methods of corroboration *and* gave him the same bloodhound approach in the search for facts that you have for investments."

Nick sneered. "Ghosts aren't quite as black-and-white as balance sheets."

"Which is exactly why we need someone of Evan's impeccable background."

Boy, if Valerie had ever dared to speak to her mother in that tone, she'd have gotten a slap for her insolence. That Nick felt free enough to speak truthfully without fearing dismissal or a dressing-down said something about the depth of their relationship. Was that it? Was he secure in his position at Moongate because Rita treated him like a son? Would he lose all that if Valentina were to come back and claim her rightful place? Something to ponder.

"I've written in-depth articles for several scientific magazines." Evan bent down to the well-worn leather messenger bag at his feet and drew out a handful of papers. "I've brought reprints. I want to record information faithfully for its scientific value." He grinned sheepishly and half rose out of the wing chair to hand Nick the articles. "I'm also fascinated by the stories I hear from the ghosts through mediums. Knowing what happened to them helps me understand the energy they left behind."

"Oh, great," Nick mumbled, discarding Evan's articles on a nearby side table. "Just what we need, a medium to add to this zoo."

Evan put a hand up. "No, no. I only bring in a medium if circumstances point to a haunting."

Nick chuffed. "Like that's not going to happen with Rita Meadows involved."

Evan's cheeks quivered. "I don't let a name, or lack of one, influence my findings."

Nick skewered him with his death-laser gaze, and, when Evan squirmed, Valerie was glad that, for once, she wasn't the recipient. "How about money? Do you let that influence the extent of your research?"

"That's quite enough, Nicolas."

"As a matter of fact, no." Evan recoiled as if insulted. "I don't charge anything to investigate a possible occurrence. My expenses are all covered by a grant."

Nick didn't look convinced. "What's the catch?"

"The catch is that I use my findings in my scientific papers."

A muscle jumped in Nick's jaw as if he were literally biting back his words.

Rita withdrew a handkerchief from the pocket of her gray wool skirt and dabbed at the pearls of sweat strung along her forehead.

"Are you all right?" Valerie poured Rita a glass of ice water from the pitcher on the silver tray.

"I'm fine, dear." Rita accepted the glass from Valerie, but didn't sip. "Evan's agreed to look at the tower room and run some tests."

"The tower room?" Valerie asked. Rita didn't look well at all. "Valentina's room?"

"There have been sounds, like a baby crying coming from the tower room, and I'd like to find out if there's a physical cause for the phenomenon." She looked pointedly at Nick.

No wonder she hadn't told Nick of her plans. Having a television crew interviewing Rita was bad enough, but a paranormal researcher had to grate against everything Nick stood for.

Having a ghost haunt the tower room would certainly put an interesting spin on the story, though. Valerie would have to corner Evan when Nick wasn't around and ask if she could tape some of his experiments for her segment.

"And if there is a poor lost soul wandering the tower room…" Rita's glass shook in her hands, clinking the ice cubes like skeleton teeth. With an awkward two-handed movement, she slid the glass on the coffee table. "Then it would be nice for him to find his way home."

His, she'd said, not her. Whoever Rita thought was haunting the tower room, she was certain it wasn't her daughter. Did Moongate hold another secret tight in its walls? How this experiment played out would certainly prove interesting.

"I suppose that's where the medium comes in," Nick grumbled.

"Evan's work is a plausible avenue for truth," Rita insisted. She raised her handkerchief to her mouth and coughed twice.

At Rita's distress, Nick crouched at her side and his whole face softened. The transformation took Valerie's breath away.

Nick, Nick, Nick, her heart sang as if he were a long-lost friend, and she had to put a hand to her chest to stop the wild gallop.

A warm smile graced Rita's lips. Her hand reached up to touch Nick's. "I know you're trying to protect me, but sometimes, you try too hard."

"You certainly don't make my job easy." Worry lines crimped Nick's forehead, and he studied the rose pattern on the carpet for a long time before looking up at Rita. "What if Gardner and his scientific methods find that the ghost is Valentina, won't that prove that Valentina is dead?"

The gentleness in his voice made Valerie want to reach for him. The longing was so strong she nearly wept out loud.

What was it about this house that turned her from a professional to an emotional wreck? What made her good at her job was her ability to remain a neutral observer. These dramatic shifts of emotions weren't like her at all.

"This is important to me, Nicolas." Rita's voice caught in her throat. "It's going to generate leads to find Valentina."

Nick raked a hand through his hair and glanced at Evan, hard mask back in place. "What exactly are your plans, Dr. Gardner?"

"I'll need to set up some equipment in the tower room where Rita has heard the cries. I've brought it all with me. It's out in my truck." Evan prattled on, completely unaware of Nick's scorn. "The people most likely to see a ghost are those who have recently suffered the loss of a loved one, are considered insane, are closer to nature and farther from cities or technology, or inhabit the sites of wrongful deaths."

Rita's cough came back with a vengeance. She clamped both hands over her chest as if to keep her lungs in. The choking gasps of her coughs made her breaths wheeze. Nick, still crouched beside her, tried to soothe her by rubbing her back.

"I'm...all right," Rita said, but as she attempted to stand, her legs gave out, and she passed out in Nick's arms.

Valerie jumped up to help, but Nick had the situation in hand. He eased Rita back to the sofa. "Rita?"

A gurgling sound came from Rita's lungs and her eyes fluttered open. Her feverish gaze locked with Valerie's. Her trembling hand reached desperately forward. "Valentina..."

Not knowing what else to do, Valerie dipped a damask napkin in the pitcher of water, wrung it and dabbed it on Rita's sweaty forehead. "I'm Valerie Zea, Ms. Meadows. From your uncle's station."

"Valentina." Rita smiled, her hot and damp hand wrapping around Valerie's wrist. Her voice was a raspy, breakable thing that hitched along Valerie's heart. "I always knew you'd come home."

THAT DID IT. Nick slipped his arms around Rita and lifted her off the sofa. Cripes, she was boiling hot and shivering. He was taking her out of here. Now. The stress of the upcoming anniversary, all of her secret plans, all these energy vampires wanting to suck her dry had driven her past the point of exhaustion. He'd been accommodating because she was Rita, but enough was enough. "Out. All of you."

"The equipment?" that quack Gardner asked.

"Later."

"I—" Valerie sputtered, standing one fist pressed to her stomach. The healthy sun-kissed glow of her skin paled three shades. Questions and apologies rounded her eyes. And God help him, he almost believed the act.

"It's the fever," Nick said. Though why he'd want to ease her guilty conscience, he didn't know. "Her calling you Valentina doesn't mean anything."

Valerie nodded. "This sounds like more than a cold."

Pneumonia, if he was right. She'd probably caught it on her secret trip to Chicago. How could she have sneaked away like that without telling him?

"I knew." Rita's voice was a hollow rasp. Her breath puffed dragon-hot against his shoulder. "I knew you'd come home."

He should've put his foot down when he'd seen how pale Rita had looked that morning, and insisted she see a doctor instead of entertaining guests of dubious intentions.

"Is there anything I can do?" Valerie placed the fingers of one hand on his elbow. The touch jolted through his system as it had yesterday. Static electricity. This old house was full of it. He'd have to ask Lionel to crank up the humidifier.

The genuine concern in Valerie's eyes added another kick to his gut, and he deliberately stepped away. "I think it would be best if you both left."

Valerie nodded, took in a shuddering breath and exhaled slowly. "I'll come back later."

"No!" Rita's weak cry gurgled. A series of jagged coughs convulsed her frail body. Nick tried to absorb the recoil of her spasms into his own chest. "Valentina…has to stay."

"Let's see what the doctor says first."

Rita banged a feeble fist against Nick's chest. "Nicolas…"

"Shh, Rita." She needed a doctor. She needed medicine. She needed them both right now. Without waiting to see if Valerie or Gardner followed his order to leave, he carried Rita to her bed and propped pillows behind her back to ease the stress on her lungs.

His mother hurried into the room. "How is she?"

"She's spiking a fever. And she passed out in the library." Seeing Rita so weak and frail burned an ache in his chest. She'd always been so strong. The first time he'd seen a picture of the Statue of Liberty, Nick had thought it was Rita. *"That's me, all right,"* she'd said, laughing. *"Hostess extraordinaire."*

"Call Dr. Marzan."

This was Valerie's fault. Hers and that Gardner quack. The stink of their conspiracy made him want to spit nails. They were ganging up, hitting all of Rita's weak spots. Her, with her Valentina looks. Him, with his false promise of an answer about the ghost. Nick would be the one who'd have to pick up all the broken pieces.

He didn't want to hurt Rita, but he couldn't let them return. She'd hate him for a while, but once she was well again, once November arrived, she'd see it was for the best. That Valentina's anniversary was better left uncommemorated. Nothing good would come from reliving the past. He should know. He'd wasted too much of his life looking for something that didn't want to be found.

"What did the doctor say?" Nick asked when his mother returned.

"He'll be here in ten minutes." Holly wrapped a cool cloth over Rita's forehead, and Rita moaned.

Nick nodded. "Watch her. I'll make sure our guests have left and show Dr. Marzan up."

He'd have to call the middle school, too. Let them know he wouldn't be able to make it today. He hated to disappoint the kids. The math tutoring sessions were his treasured hours of sunshine every week, and he looked forward to them as much as the kids did.

Rita caught the material of Nick's jacket as he tried to leave. "You have to…promise me, Nicolas."

"Rita—"

"No, you have to…promise." She hacked, the fluid in her lungs giving her voice a wet, strangled sound. "Valentina has to…stay."

Nick shook his head. "I can't allow—"

Face set, Rita turned to Holly. "You can cancel…that call to Dr. Marzan. I refuse…to see him."

"Your health is—"

"It's my mind…my heart that need…healing."

Rita's body curved to catch the blow of another round of coughing. Holly sat beside her, supporting her.

"I won't let you do this to yourself." Nick balled his fists at his sides. "I'll call an ambulance and force you to get care."

"You're my only link…to Valentina, Nicolas. I would hate to…lose you. But if you can't support me…" Silent tears twisted down her flame-red cheeks. "Then you'd better…pack your bags…because I never want…to see you again."

Holly sucked in a breath as she held the coughing Rita. "You don't mean that, Rita."

"I do. I want…Valentina home."

"She's not Valentina," Nick said between gritted teeth. Seeing Rita so sick, so delusional from her fever, tore him to pieces.

"Nicky, just do it," Holly pleaded, her eyes filled with the kind of fear he hadn't seen there in a long time. "Just do as she says. What harm can there be? She needs care, and she needs it now. Give her something to fight for."

Every fiber of his being screamed at him to put an end to this farce. Kick the pseudo-Valentina and the paranormal quack out the door and let life return to normal. But once Rita made up her mind, there was no changing it. And if she lost her will to live, this illness could kill her.

There was no winning. Letting the headline hunters exploit the family's privacy was a crime. But so was killing Rita's hope when she'd given him and his mother so much.

Nick nodded once. For now, he'd give in. When Rita's fever broke, she'd see she'd made a mistake. "I can invite her, but I can't force her to stay."

Rita attempted to squeeze his hand, but her grip was nothing more than a flutter against his palm. "Convince her, Nicolas."

"ARE YOU COMPLETELY LOONY?" Valerie asked, one arm crossed over the portfolio she held close to her chest, her free hand clutching her half-filled cup of coffee.

As Mike was finishing up loading his camera in the trunk, Nick had caught her and hauled her back inside. They were now standing in the foyer, their voices rebounding off the ceiling as if they stood in an echo chamber, adding a macabre note to their insane exchange. His crazy proposal hammered against everything she believed in.

"Trust me," he said. "I'd just as soon run you out of town as invite you into our home."

"I can't lie."

"Not even for your story?"

She hesitated. "I have other avenues for research."

"But none so complete and accurate."

He had a point. Rita had information from her dealings with the police and private investigators that Valerie could never get her hands on in the time she had to put the package together. Her promotion depended on her doing not just a good job, but a great job with this project. A project that would bear extra scrutiny because of the station owner's personal interest.

Then there was the time issue. With Rita sick, an interview with her was out of the question.

Which didn't leave her with many options.

To complete her assignment, she'd have to compromise her previously impeccable ethics. What did that say about her? About the depth of her ambition? Was that the first step to fabricating news?

Nick scoffed. "Think of it as immersion into your role."

"I can't do this. I can't pretend I'm Valentina. I wouldn't know how. It's not right. And you, of all people, shouldn't be asking this of me."

He stepped closer, his eyes blazing down at her. His presence pulsated along her skin, making her wish she'd put on the V-neck cashmere sweater she'd gotten on clearance under her blazer. He could cut through too many layers with that look, and she didn't like the way she wanted to swat him as a kid would and say, *Stop it, Nick. That's not funny.*

"Not even to help a sick woman recover? Your employer's niece?" His voice slid seductively into her brain matter, making the walls of the foyer waver once again. "What's a few days when you could have such easy access to your target?"

"Interview." She readjusted her grip on her portfolio, sliding it up to shield her throat. "I don't know why you keep insisting I'm trying to swindle Ms. Meadows out of anything."

His hands reached for her shoulders. Their possessive weight burned right through her blazer, blouse and camisole and down to her skin. "Val…"

The abbreviation of her name, spoken so softly, seemed to pluck at something deep and faraway, something so familiar that it made her heart ache and her throat close up.

"Rita is sick," he said. "She needs a reason to fight for her health. These past few years have been especially hard on her." For an instant his eyes showed the truth of his words and his worry softened the hard lines of his face. Just as fast, the iron gates of his control fell back into place, closing off her glimpse into his soul. "You want your story?"

Not trusting her voice, she nodded.

"Then make up your mind. *Now*."

She didn't want to, but she yielded. She had no choice. Not if she was going to complete her assignment successfully.

"I'll stay," she said, unwilling to capitulate completely, "but only if you agree to allow me to interview you in Rita's place."

Before Nick could reply, a long scream rent the air. He took off up the stairs. Propelled by curiosity, Valerie followed, cementing her deal with the devil. For the story, she'd play Valentina.

In a small office in shades of cream and gray, the woman with the braid stood behind a nineteenth-century English writing table. Both of her trembling hands covered her mouth, squashing down further screams that might disturb Rita. Her brown eyes, wide and petrified, stared at something hidden behind the raised cover of a laptop.

Cautiously, Valerie moved to get a better view. Nick reached down to the keyboard and, with the tip of a pencil, picked up the gold chain snaked across the keys. The gold hissed like a cobra as it rose and an oval cameo dangled from its end. The profile, etched on moonstone, was that of a little girl.

As the edge of the cameo whispered across the touch pad, the screen came to life. In seventy-point font, red letters proclaimed, "I know where she is."

Chapter Five

Valentina's face dangled from the cameo like a hypnotist's focus point. The milky profile spinning on its chain unwound the years. Nick longed to grasp the moonstone and fist it in his hand. Would it still heat his palm?

Valentina. His heart wrenched just looking at the stone. A birthday present from her father carved by a local artist. Her pixie profile caught in all its mischief and sunshine.

It itches, she'd said and discarded the expensive bauble along with her party dress, fancy shoes and ribbons and slipped into flannel pajamas and fuzzy socks.

He closed his eyes against the memory. *Don't think.*

Where had this necklace come from? Who'd had access to Rita's office? Who'd had the gall to write such a button-pushing note?

Thank God Rita hadn't found it.

I know where she is. Those simple words would have Rita demanding he turn the earth inside out. As if he hadn't already done it a dozen times.

He wasn't a big believer in coincidence, either. What

were the chances that something like this would happen when three strangers were running around the mansion? You didn't have to be a whiz at probs and stats to know they were off the charts and that the culprit was probably in the house.

He'd fought so hard to keep Rita safe, but the crazies had still found a way in.

Aware of his audience, he opened his eyes again, control back in place. He doubted whoever had planted the necklace on Rita's computer had bothered to leave fingerprints behind, but he couldn't take a chance. With a look to Holly, he silently asked if she was all right.

She hitched in a breath, nodded and said, "I'll call the detective."

"Make sure the photographer and the professor stick around."

She nodded once and left.

"What is it?" Valerie scratched at the base of her throat. Her gaze fixated on the stone as if puzzled and searching for an answer just out of reach.

He plucked an envelope from the drawer in Rita's desk and let the moonstone drop inside. "Nothing of importance."

"Is it Valentina's? Was she wearing it on the night she disappeared?"

The curiosity breezing through Valerie's voice almost made him smile. *What happens next, Nick? Tell me more.* Valentina could never get enough of the stories he'd woven to entertain her.

Stay focused. No way to tell who'd crept upstairs to leave the message. Even in a hurry, any fool who'd watched television knew enough to wear gloves. And discarded latex gloves could easily fit in a pocket or a purse.

Lionel was with the photographer, but the photographer could have made an excuse and escaped long enough to plant the necklace. And the quack and Valerie both had a chance to do the same while he and his mother were with Rita.

The way things were going, the tower ghost was just as likely to have dropped the necklace on the keyboard and used telekinesis or whatever crap ghosts used to move objects to type the freaking note.

If he couldn't keep the crazies out, he had to keep them in and contain them.

Using the eraser end of the pencil, he pressed the print button and made two color copies of the message—one for his files and one for the detective who still handled Valentina's case.

"Ambition is usually an admirable quality," he said. "But not when it hurts others."

Valerie looked him square in the eye with an intensity that threw him for a second. "Ambition is only part of what drives me. I do my job well. I'm good at it. No, make that great. The best. I tell stories that show the resiliency of spirit, the beauty of place, the importance of things, their history." Her palms rose and she shook her head. "You can't think I did this."

"I'm reserving judgment."

She raised an eyebrow that said, Oh yeah? "Well, that's a first. Does that mean I'm off the bad-guy list?"

"No."

She tipped her head, watching him as if she could read him. "Why are you fighting so hard against answers? Don't you want to know?"

The million-dollar question. Easy for her to ask. Impossible for him to answer. Yes, he wanted to know where Valentina's body was hidden. Needed to know. He squeezed the back of his neck. But the answer would leave no gray ground, no hope, and he feared the knowing would destroy Rita.

"You're just doing your job," he said, more as a reminder to himself than to placate her. "I still have to do mine."

Her smile brightened the bleak room. "Wow. I accept."

He shot her a questioning glance.

"Your apology. I accept."

He frowned away the unexpected wave of warmth and searched the desk for errant clues. "I was making a simple observation."

A crunching noise drew his attention outside where a black sedan rolled up the driveway. Clout had its benefits. A cold case like Valentina's could still get you a detective's visit in less than fifteen minutes. "Why don't you go down to the library? I'll have Holly show you the archives."

She turned slowly and made her way across the carpet. His mind's eye rolled back the years, seeing a bratty three-year-old in her place, hands stuffed in her jeans pockets, scuffing the tip of her sneaker on the carpet because he didn't want to play with her.

At the door, Valerie craned her head over her shoulder. The dove-gray wall contoured the curves of her figure in the navy pencil skirt and fitted blazer. Definitely not a little girl.

"I understand that you don't want Valentina's story to be voyeurism, you know," she said.

"The jury's still out."

She threw her head back and the ripple of her laughter skimmed against him like light on water. "I'm so relieved. I thought you'd appointed yourself sole judge and executioner. A jury, I can handle."

"HERE YOU ARE." Holly opened the door to a room on the second floor after dinner that night. As far away from Rita's quarters as possible, Valerie noticed.

"Thank you." Valerie placed the bag, which Mike had retrieved from the inn for her, at the foot of the bed.

"The bathroom's through that door." Holly dropped a pile of fresh towels on the bed. "I'll leave you alone."

But she didn't. She got as far as the door, then stood there, watching. And her presence pressed down Valerie's neck like a vampire testing for a good artery, giving her a case of the creeps. "Don't get too comfortable. This isn't permanent."

Holly didn't mean to pick on her specifically, Valerie rationalized. She would treat any other person who'd invaded the mansion the same way. To protect Rita. Same as Nick. Mike and Evan had probably suffered through the same warning. Valerie caught herself toying with the hem of her blazer, then knitted her fingers together in front of her and cleared her throat. "Mike and I will be leaving on Friday."

"See that you do."

After Holly left, her steps spookily silent on the hallway runner, Valerie sat on the edge of the bed, alone in the dark, except for the light from the hallway.

The guest room was filled with cozy antiques that invited relaxation. A small pitcher of water covered with an upside-down glass that did double duty as a stopper rested on the night table beside the Brighton brothel bed, draped with a blue-and-white diamond-pattern quilt. An overstuffed blue-and-white French toile chair was angled to give the sitter a perfect view of Mount Monadnock outside. A collage of blue butterflies on a translucent background that looked like frosted glass rested above the cherry dresser.

But that's where the coziness ended. No heat seemed to reach the room. Valerie removed her blazer and dug through her bag for her bright pink fleece hoodie.

Through the lace-covered window the moon hung huge and silver against a sky the color of dead coals. The sound of tree branch tips scratching against the glass crawled around the room like spiders. The plaintive howl of a faraway dog, filled with hopelessness that whatever it wanted wasn't going to be granted, reminded Valerie of her neurotic dog and home.

She sighed. She should call her mother, see how she and said neurotic dog were getting along. But not yet. Valerie wasn't in the mood for a lecture, or worse, pleas to come home right away to take care of some sort of imagined emergency that seemed to crop up only when Valerie was out of town. For a woman with such uncompromising strength, her mother's clinginess when it came to her only child confused Valerie.

Which brought her thoughts back to Rita. The doctor had come and gone. Rita had refused to go to the hospital, so he'd rigged up an IV and left a long list of instructions and the suggestion Nick hire a nurse. On one hand, Rita's illness would mean very little contact with her, so Valerie's deception would be minimal. On the other, doing her job would be more difficult. Nick would make a rotten interview. So would Holly. Which meant she'd have to find another way to get Valentina's story across in a way that would please Rita—and hopefully, help her recover her health.

Valerie would rather be back at the inn where the atmosphere wasn't so thick. Where it would be easier to think creatively. Where Nick's strong personality and her odd attraction to the man lost some of its urgency. Not attraction, that was too strong. Curiosity? That was more like it. She was curious at the pull he seemed to have on her, at the reason why her mind kept swimming into Valentina's photo album when he was around.

Coming here was wrong. She didn't like to get emotionally involved with the subjects of her segments. She needed to keep a certain distance to put together a fair and balanced portrait. How could she do that when she was living a lie? She threw herself back on the pillows and closed her eyes.

Her phone rang. Groaning, Valerie answered it. *Entertainment Tonight* or *Extra* or another of the celebrity gossip shows her mother favored blasted in the background.

"Valerie?" her mother practically shouted. "You sound tired."

Tired? No, more like confused and frustrated. She'd accomplished almost nothing since she'd arrived. "Long day, Mom."

Her mother clucked. "I told you that you don't need that job. It takes too much out of you, and it takes you too far from home."

"I love what I do, Mom."

"If you'd gone to nursing school like I'd suggested, you could've married a doctor by now, and I could have a couple of grandchildren to spoil."

"Mom—"

"When are you coming home?"

"I told you. Friday night. Late."

"I hope they pay you overtime for all that travel."

"They pay me just fine." A joke, actually, especially for all the hours she put in.

"What did you do today?"

Growing up, Valerie had had to account for every minute of her life. Arriving even five minutes late would send her mother into such a spin that Valerie had learned promptness at an early age. She'd thought that, once she was out on her own, her mother would finally ease up, but if anything, her mother seemed to equate getting on an airplane and flying to New Hampshire on a par with banishment to Siberia.

But now, seeing the devastation of Valentina's loss on Rita Meadows, Valerie could almost understand her mother's tight clutch. Especially since Daddy had died in a freak accident at the garage he'd owned.

Valerie sat up, feet solidly on the ground. "I read through the archives the Meadowses have collected over the years."

"Did you find anything interesting?"

Valerie imagined her mother sitting back in the recliner in Valerie's living room, settling in for a long chat. "A couple of possible interviews, but no, not much that was new." Disappointing, really.

"So you'll be home Friday."

"Yes, Mom. Friday."

An annoying gum commercial played in the background.

"So, how is she? Ms. Meadows?" her mother asked, hesitation causing speed bumps in her voice. "Do you like her?"

"She's like you'd expect, Mom. Devastated by her loss, but still full of hope that one day her daughter will come home. Actually, she got sick today, and I ended up getting an invitation to stay at Moongate for a couple of days." No way was she going to tell her mother about Rita mistaking her for Valentina.

Her mother gasped. "You're at the mansion?"

Her mother was always warning Valerie about the temptations of this world, of how her choice of career would lure her away from a true and humble path. Mom wasn't big on organized religion—just the corrupting temptations of wealth and the evil of money. Valerie tried to mollify her. "It looks just like one of those fancy decorating magazines, cold and impersonal. It's definitely not as cozy as home."

"Remember where you're from, the values we've taught you."

In the background, Valerie's dog started to yip, her mother to sob.

"Mom? Are you okay?"

"You have to come home, Valerie."

Here we go. "The job's not over."

"Can't you hear the racket? I can't control her."

Her was Luna, short for Lunatic. Something wasn't quite right with the dog. Valerie had found the basenji yodeling at the night sky, trapped in some illegally dumped garbage off the trail where Valerie ran every day. No one had answered the lost-dog ad or the posters she'd placed, and realizing that Luna's nasty habit made her un-adoptable, Valerie hadn't had the heart to turn her in at the animal shelter.

"She won't shut up." Her mother's grief sounded all out of proportion to the situation. "The neighbors are threat-ening to call the cops."

Wouldn't be the first time. "It's the moon, it drives her crazy. Hang something over the slider windows so she can't see out."

"She won't let me anywhere near her."

Valerie huffed out a breath and ran a hand through her hair. "She weighs twenty pounds, Mom. How hard can it be to push by her?"

"You know, if you're going to take on the responsibility of a dog, you need to be home to take care of her."

Luna's yips turned into full-bore yodels as if someone was encouraging her. "Put her on the phone."

Her mother's hysteria died down for a moment. "You want me to put a dog on the phone?"

"You want the racket to end?"

"All right."

"Luna!" The lament stopped midsong and was followed by a happy yip of recognition, and Valerie smiled as she imagined Luna's permanent quizzical expression. "You need to be on your best behavior, understand?"

"Urf." Luna's red corkscrew tail thumped against a chair leg in Valerie's kitchen.

"I mean it. I don't want to find your corpse lying on the kitchen floor when I come back."

"Urf."

"Trust me, when it comes to Mom, there's no contest. Even if you hold up your end of the battle of wills, you'll come out bloody and battered."

Which was why Valerie had been loath to ask her mother for a favor in the middle of a disagreement. But she couldn't leave Luna alone, and none of the local kennels would take her because of the moon thing. Even the vet had joked that Luna must be part Swiss werewolf the way the sight of the moon set her off on a yodeling jag.

Valerie didn't know who she felt more sorry for—her crazy dog or her mother.

"Mom!" Valerie waited until her mother came back on. "I think Luna'll be fine. Just hang a sheet or something over the door. Or take her in the bedroom with you."

"I'm not risking getting fleas."

"Your choice."

"You have to come home, Valerie."

"I can't, Mom, not yet."

"I gave you a life. Doesn't that count for anything?"

And her mother called her melodramatic! Where did

she think Valerie had learned it? "It counts for a lot, Mom. But you're the one who told me to always finish what I start."

The gossip show's theme music thumped with heavy bass in the background.

"Valerie?" Her mother gulped as if she'd just swum a mile. "Remember that I love you."

Valerie sighed. "I know, Mom. I love you, too."

A noise. No, more like a sensation of heat at the back of her neck made her turn around. Nick's looming six-foot frame filled the doorway. "I have to go. I'll talk to you later."

HE SHOULDN'T HAVE COME. This could've waited till morning. But he'd been thinking of her, couldn't seem to lock her out of his head, so he'd made the detour to her room before heading up to the carriage house that was his home and finishing the day's business.

She looked small perched on the bed edge as if she were ready to flee. One hand, long-fingered and delicate, gripped the blue-and-white quilt with a fist that didn't appear strong enough to harm a butterfly. Her big blue eyes had the look of a lost little girl.

He didn't want to hold her, he told himself. Didn't want to comfort her. The twitch in his hands, the tensing of his muscles were from the hard day that had gone on much too long and still had hours to go.

He needed to remember that there was strength in that slim body. The kind of strength that rang all of his alarm bells. The kind of strength he couldn't afford to underestimate. Whatever she stirred in him, it had to stop. He forced himself to unknot his muscles and lean against the door frame as if her presence in this house was normal.

She dropped her cell phone in the purse at her feet, filled a glass with water from the pitcher and looked up at him, trying to look casual. But her eyes gave her away.

"Did you want something?" Her fingers played a nervous tune against the glass.

"I wanted to make sure you were settled in all right."

Half her mouth curved up mischievously. "Are you going to lock me in to make sure I don't wander out alone?"

The beginning of a smile tugged at his lips. "Do I need to?"

She sipped and made a face. "The water." She touched her mouth with three fingers. "It tastes funny."

"Well water. You'll get used to the mineral taste."

She pursed her lips and nodded, but slid the glass back onto the night table. "Was there anything else?"

"When is your interview with Kirby Cicco tomorrow?" The creep and his two friends were hired to help with the party preparations on the day of Valentina's disappearance. They'd come back that night and taken off with Rita's jewelry and, according to the evidence, her daughter.

Valerie reached for a decorative pillow and clamped it over her chest with crossed arms, hands hanging on to the tassels on each corner.

"Here comes the scary part," Nick whispered to Valentina as they watched forbidden cartoons.

Valentina reached for a pink pillow and used it as a shield. Eyes shut tight, she squeezed closer to him. "Tell me when it's over."

He'd never have admitted it, but he'd liked it when she'd turned to him, when all he'd needed to do to make her feel safe was wrap an arm around her shoulders.

"How did you—" Valerie started, jolting him back to the present.

"What time?" Nick asked with a harsher tone than he'd meant. He stuck his hands in his pockets.

Valerie squished the pillow tighter, her eyes wide with question. "Ten. The prison official I talked to said it was a couple hours' drive from here. Why?"

"I'll drive. Be ready at seven-thirty."

She opened her mouth to argue, but he spun on his heel and left. Not, he assured himself, because he was afraid she could change his mind—nothing was going to stop him from going with her on that interview—but because every time he looked at her a mad whirlwind of memories threatened to engulf him, and the last thing he wanted to do was to reach out to her.

Chapter Six

"Can you stop at the next exit?" Valerie asked him as a highway sign with a food icon slipped by.

Nick didn't know why he was so ticked off that everything about her had checked out—at least on the surface. He'd told Joe to keep digging until he'd turned over every last rock in her life. No word yet on Simon Higgins's financial status or Gordon Archer's whereabouts—other than the news that Gordon had been a guest of the Florida state prison system as recently as last year. Why didn't that surprise Nick in the least?

Coming face-to-face with the man in prison for kidnapping Valentina was just one more tug into a place he didn't want to revisit.

"You're trying to stall again." Nick concentrated on the road, thick with leaf-peepers even though the season was petering out. What was the point of owning a Jaguar with a supercharged V-8 and four hundred horses if you were stuck doing thirty in a fifty-five zone? Just a touch of the accelerator and this baby could move, and boy, did he want to floor it and let her rip. "We're going to be late."

"If Mike doesn't get fed, things will get ugly."

"And if she doesn't get coffee," Mike added from the backseat and made an exaggerated shivering noise. "You don't want to be around."

"She's already had two cups. And if you wanted breakfast, you should've gotten up earlier." They called themselves professionals?

"Trust me," Mike grumbled. "You want to get her topped off. And I work better on a full stomach."

A whorl of blue trooper lights and red fire truck lights and a twist of metal between a minivan and a Toyota blocked the exit and saved him from another argument—and a stop. He just wanted to get this ordeal over and done with. "Accident. You'll both have to wait."

Valerie kept fighting him every mile of the way up to the North Country, which kept him from obsessing and, strangely enough, calmed him.

"You're not cleared," she insisted even now at the prison's doors. "We got special permission to come on a nonvisiting day and interview Mr. Cicco." She backhanded the letter. "Interviewer and photog only."

"I'll get in." The many ways the Meadows name opened doors never ceased to amaze him.

"Have you ever *been* to a prison?" she asked, as if he didn't know what he was getting himself into.

"Not recently. Have you?"

"Well, actually, no." She stopped and turned to him, mouth hanging open. "Wait. You've been to a prison? When? Why?"

Before he could answer, their escort arrived and they

were buzzed, beeped and clanged through doors, then stripped of anything that a prisoner could turn into a weapon.

The acrid smell of despair and anger underlying the antiseptic made Nick's nose twitch. But it was the ceaseless noise, like the raspy breath of evil on a moonless night, that always got to him, put him on edge.

"What did you do?" Valerie whispered. The erratic echo of their heels and the stark light, arcing off the walls, gave the corridor the fractured feeling of an alien world. "Bribe a prison official?"

"I went straight to the governor," he teased.

She narrowed her eyes at him. "You can't mess this up for me."

"Why would I?"

"Well, I don't know. Could be your charming disposition and your death-laser glare. He's not going to want to talk to me with you intimidating him. And my segment's already compromised with Rita sick and you not worth my bother to interview."

"You find me intimidating?" he asked, doing his best to ignore the way the corridor seemed to lengthen and snake endlessly or the way he wanted to grab her hand and hold on tight.

She touched her chest with her fingertips. "Me? No. But I suspect most people do."

"Why don't I intimidate you?" Needling her kept the toxic wash of adrenaline from eating into him.

She tilted her head. "Could we focus here? I'm working. This is my job. It's important to me. You know— on par with you keeping pretenders out of Rita's way."

"You do fluff pieces."

"Well, I'm flattered. You checked up on me. But if you'd bothered to watch a whole segment, you'd know that I provide a deeper insight."

Yeah, he knew. And her ability to get to the heart of a person in a few minutes had surprised him. He'd found himself savoring the lingering feel-good button she'd pushed.

More clanging and banging and reverberating echoes jangled his nerves as they were led into the visitors' room where the air threatened to collapse under the weight of broken dreams and failed promises. What had made him think time had erased the density of misery?

Valerie consulted with Mike and they chose a table in the middle of the stagnant space. She deposited a file of notes on the surface while Mike set up his gear.

She came to stand next to Nick. "I don't get why you want to be here."

"Personal reasons."

She snorted. "Yeah, let's not give too much away."

Once again he saw a three-year-old in front of him. Valentina in her overalls and pigtails, all huffy and pouty because he wasn't talking to her. He blinked away the image. "What exactly is it that you're hoping to accomplish with this interview?"

"Something you're fighting suspiciously hard—getting to the truth of what happened to Valentina."

"What makes you think one word coming out of a con's mouth is going to come anywhere near the truth?"

Nick certainly had heard none the last time he'd visited his father in prison.

Her sigh bounced in the bad acoustics of the room. "Okay, this is how it's going to work. You're going to go sit over there." She pointed at the far corner out of the prisoner's line of sight. "You're going to focus on anything, except Mr. Cicco."

Nick slid his gaze appreciatively down the length of her body. "Anything you say."

She bumped his chin back up with the edge of her hand until their gazes met and lifted a brow in warning. "You're not going to interrupt, snigger, suggest, bully or otherwise interfere with my interview." Her arm swept in front of her to point at the door. "Or I'm going to have that big guard over there throw you out." She put on her own version of his death-laser glare. "And don't think I won't."

Mike hooted. "She will, too. I've seen her do it."

Nick lifted his hands, palms up in mock surrender. "Bossy, aren't you?"

"When I'm working, yes."

A guard led in the prisoner stuffed into a jumpsuit like a salami, and Valerie turned away from Nick, all business. Mike attached a mic to the jumpsuit, then went back to his camera, and seemed to melt into the background.

Nick retreated to his assigned corner, because observing had been his intention in the first place and not because the four-foot dictator had asked him to.

A blade of anxiety stabbed him under the rib cage and wrenched the breath out of him. He'd sworn he'd never come back, never submit himself to the soul-sucking gravity of evil. But he'd had to know. To look the man in the eyes.

Cicco had gained weight since his arrest and lost hair. Really, he was nothing more than a pathetic sad sack. How could he be the source of such nightmares?

To keep his thoughts from tumbling back to the horror of that night, Nick focused on Valerie as she prepared for the interview. Watching her was like watching a ballet, and he could breathe again.

She'd gone for the competent, professional look. As if pinning her hair up in a severe bun could take away the softness of her face and divert the prisoner's attention from her femininity. Her gray tailored pantsuit had a mannish cut that couldn't quite hide the subtle curves beneath the wool. Did she wear silk under the pale pink cotton blouse? He shook his head. *Out of the gutter, Galloway.* Allowing his thoughts to run on such dangerous lines made him no better than the creep staring at her breasts.

Nick moved, drawing the convict's attention away from Valerie's chest, and sent him a silent warning. She glared at Nick over her shoulder. He gave a small nod acknowledging her admonition, but he wouldn't let that stop him from breaking Cicco's arms if he tried to move in on her.

Standing behind her, out of the way, Nick rocked on his heels and shoved his hands in his pockets so he wouldn't preemptively punch out the pervert.

His mood was edgy, and he needed it to stay even.

Kirby Cicco was serving a life sentence, but the case was still open, thanks to the family lawyer's unwavering pressure for answers. Someone from the attorney general's office worked the case on and off, but no new leads had turned up in over a decade.

"Are we ready?" Valerie asked Mike.

"We're at speed," Mike said, hidden behind the eye of his camera.

She smiled at Cicco. "Are you ready to start, Mr. Cicco?"

"Kirby." He went all gaga on her, blushing and shuffling his feet like a lovesick teenager. "Call me Kirby. And yeah, I got nothing to hide. I didn't kidnap or kill that kid."

She started with simple questions to put her subject at ease. She asked her questions in a way that their meaning would be clear to the viewer even if they didn't hear them. And the siren song of her voice made Nick want to confess to sins he hadn't committed.

"Tell me about that day, Mr. Cicco. What were you doing at Moongate Mansion?"

"There was some sort of fancy party going to happen. We—"

"Who is 'we'?"

"My buddies, Tim Vore and Derrick Thiede. We'd done some odd jobs there before, and Ms. Meadows had hired us to help the old man with some yard work."

Nick knew the story by heart. His focus on the creep's words waned, and he let the man's essence speak instead. The side-to-side snake flicker of his eyes in their sockets. The slimy tendrils of anger, the bone-gnawing hunger for retaliation, the soul-deep rot of evil.

"They didn't have nothing on me. I got railroaded."

Cicco lifted his foot and plopped it on the table. "Does that look like a nine and a half? It's a freaking size twelve!"

"Back on the ground, Cicco," the guard ordered.

Cicco flipped the guard the bird, but obeyed. "I deserve another trial, but I can't afford no fancy lawyer."

The police had combed the house for clues, but the kidnapper had left nothing behind, except a few blurred shoe prints from a pair of Nike basketball shoes. Could a moron like Cicco have left so little evidence behind?

The next morning, the police had found a blue baby blanket stained with blood in the woods behind the house along with the stub of the same brand of cigarette Cicco smoked. Nick's blanket. Valentina's blood. The pond was drained, but no body turned up.

"Where were you at the time of the kidnapping?" Valerie asked.

"I was hanging around my house, drinking beer. How was I supposed to know I'd need an alibi?"

"The police report said you and your friends had gone down to Lawrence earlier that afternoon to buy some crack."

"I'll tell you the same thing I told the cops. The real kidnapper threatened to hurt my family. My dad, he was sick, and that bastard said he was going to burn my dad's house down with him in it."

"You took a polygraph and failed."

"I was being blackmailed. No surprise I failed when I was all twisted around."

After Valentina was taken, Nick hadn't known what to do with all the big feelings boxing inside him, so he'd taken them out on Rita and his mother. In spite of their own grief, they'd never blamed him for Valentina's disappearance. For them, he'd worked hard to shape himself into a good man. He was a hard worker, a loving son, a loyal employee. He donated his time, skills and money to local causes to improve the lives of the less fortunate, just as Rita had taught him through her example.

He was a good man.

Yet the blood flowing in his veins had left a latent print he couldn't seem to escape. Watching Cicco fold the truth and rearrange it, Nick tasted a pungent craving for vengeance on his tongue. He wanted to see this man hurt, see him twist in agony, see him dead.

But if Nick gave in to his baser instincts even once, could he stop? Or would the darkness take over and continue the cycle of violence for yet another generation?

He was a good man, wasn't he?

"You were convicted of kidnapping on the strength of another inmate's testimony," Valerie continued, never once consulting her notes. That was some memory. How deeply had she studied Valentina's life? Was it only for the story's sake as she claimed? "He said you confessed to doing the crime."

"I was lying. Stupid, but I was bragging. I was trying to be this punk, you know. Tough. You can't say you're not guilty in here and expect to be left alone. I said I'd done it for survival."

Amazing how nobody ever did anything wrong, how every convict's troubles were always someone else's fault. How often had he heard that growing up? *You made me do it.*

Cicco's gaze begged understanding, and Valerie gave a small nod that neither condemned nor approved. How could she remain so unaffected?

"I mean I told the guy other lies, too," Cicco said, milking the poor-me victim act, "but those never came out. I said I'd popped a cop. I said I made drug runs for a high-volume dealer. All of it hogwash. But no, the cops and the lawyers, they just picked what they needed to cage me. That's it. I mean, what would I do with a kid?"

Kill her, then torture her poor parents with a ransom note.

"What about your friends?" Valerie asked. "How come they didn't get prosecuted along with you?"

A sneer twisted Cicco's mouth. "The cops and the lawyers, they got what they wanted. They said there wasn't enough evidence against Tim and Derrick, and they dropped the charges."

"You were offered a plea bargain of twenty-five years if you'd plead guilty and testify against the others."

"I'd be a free man if I'd taken the deal."

"Why didn't you?"

"I ain't no rat," he said, as if that was obvious.

"What happened to your friends?" Valerie asked.

"Derrick's serving four-to-ten for robbing a gas station clerk at knifepoint. Idiot. Tim's dead. Drug overdose."

Mike gestured to catch Valerie's attention, then mouthed, "Low battery. No spare."

"So the jewelry, that was for drugs?" Valerie spoke fast, trying to squeeze in a few more questions before the camera died.

"Yeah, for drugs." Cicco smiled sheepishly. "I'd seen a pile of cash in the office upstairs when I went to fix a light. I went back for that, and she'd left a tray of jewelry out. I figured she wouldn't miss 'em, and if she did, she could always buy herself more." He drummed the fingertips of both hands against the tabletop once, then stared at his palsied fingers. "It's a disease, you know, the drugs."

"I know. Valentina was still in her room when you left?"

"Never saw the kid."

Mike sliced a finger across his throat, signifying the battery had died.

"Thank you for your time."

"Ain't like I got anything better to do." Cicco rose. The guard approached. "Hey, you think you could look into that lawyer thing for me? I cooperated."

"I'm not sure there's anything I can do, Mr. Cicco."

He spat at the floor, then gave her the evil eye. "Yeah, figures."

The guard shuffled the prisoner out, and Nick kept staring after him. He'd hoped this visit would calm his fears, show him that danger was behind bars where it couldn't hurt anyone again.

Even though a six-year-old's fear fogged his memory, and even though all adults appeared like giants in a kid's eyes, some part of him understood the monster that haunted him had grown in size over the years.

Cicco wasn't the man who'd stolen Valentina.

But he'd suspected as much since he'd read the trial transcripts, hadn't he?

"How could you forget a spare battery?" Valerie chided Mike as he dismantled his equipment.

"My mind was fogged by lack of food."

Valerie gathered her file while Mike hiked his equipment to his shoulder. "Let's get out of here."

Morning had bled into afternoon, stippling the asphalt with dislocating shadows and turning the prison windows into white squares of fire. The biting odor of dying autumn leaves sharpened the crisp air and cut right through Nick's jacket. His muscles were tight and he couldn't quite breathe right, wouldn't until they left the prison grounds and the building was just a dot in the rearview mirror.

Somewhere outside these walls, evil was watching, waiting to strike. Nick couldn't shake the certainty that it would storm Moongate again. Maybe already had. That, this time, he would lose more than his only true friend.

He couldn't wait to hit the soccer field tonight. Kicking a ball around always cleared his head, made him see things more clearly.

"You okay?" Valerie asked as he helped Mike stow his equipment in the trunk of the Jag.

"Never better. You?"

She shrugged, but couldn't quite hide that the evil inside the prison had touched her. "I'm good."

"If you're planning on doing hard-hitting news, you're going to have to grow a thicker skin."

"My skin's just fine, thanks."

He'd noticed. And he very much wanted to touch it, taste it, lose himself in the warm sweetness of it until he forgot all about the darkness inside him, waiting to erupt and destroy him.

But seeking solace there would put him straight into enemy arms. The one place he needed to avoid if he was going to get to the truth.

BY FOUR IN THE AFTERNOON, Mount Monadnock already shadowed Moonhill into dusk. Violet and orange veined the horizon. The ball of sun burned like a weak candle, pale yellow and diffuse against the mountain's summit. And the charcoal blanket of night unfurled along its eastern slope.

They'd stopped for a late lunch, and Valerie had hoped the greasy food she'd forced down would camouflage the vile scent of prison that clung to her clothes like stale cigarette smoke. Even the take-out French vanilla coffee she held under her nose as Nick drove up Windemere Drive didn't help. She'd need a long, hot shower and soap, lots of soap.

And she'd need to talk to Higgins.

"We'll have to stay," she said to no one in particular, already drawing up a mental to-do list.

"Hey, no can do," Mike piped in from the back. "I've got a date on Saturday. Can't break it."

When you worked ten-hour-plus days, the pool of potential mates was pretty much limited to coworkers who worked the same crazy hours, and Valerie had seen Mike hang around the new intern. "She'll understand."

Valerie's mother would have a fit, though. So would Holly, who hadn't wanted them to stay there in the first place.

"You don't understand," Mike whined. "This is serious. And she's not in the business."

"This could be big, Mike. That man didn't kidnap Valentina."

Valerie had come away from the prison visit with the certainty that though Kirby Cicco probably did belong in jail for a long list of reasons, kidnapping Valentina wasn't one of them. His profession of innocence wasn't what convinced her. It was more the narrow scope of his focus. His history of crime ran along petty lines. Nothing to say he couldn't escalate, just that she didn't think he had the fortitude to carry out such a complex plan. The night he'd crept back to Moongate, he'd wanted a quick fix, not a big payoff.

And she'd bet a week's worth of coffee that Nick had come away with the same conclusion, and that was why he was so gloomy and silent.

But if Kirby Cicco hadn't taken Valentina, then Valentina's kidnapper could still be running free. And if she could unearth new evidence, then maybe Valentina could finally come home and give Rita some peace. Not to mention that Valerie could get the break she needed to launch her career to the next level.

"Just how did you jump to that conclusion?" Nick asked. His profile cut sharp edges in the car's dim interior. Why were the lines of his face so familiar? Why did her hands want to reach for him, her head to lean against his shoulder?

"Same way you did," Valerie said. "I looked into his eyes."

"No wonder they keep you doing fluff pieces."

Nick stopped at the iron gates to the mansion and

pressed the gate opener. The gates swung open, allowing them through. Long claws of shade crawled along the road, turning it black.

Nick picked up speed on the driveway.

"I'll have you know—"

Something jumped out from behind the trees.

"What was that?" Valerie asked.

"Holy moly," Mike said.

Nick stomped on the brakes, but he couldn't stop in time and the tires bumped over the dark shape.

"Oh, my God!" Valerie crammed her coffee cup in a cup holder and reached for the door handle with both hands. "You hit an animal or something. Stop the car!"

She jumped out and ran to the rear of the car. She crouched by the lump, a macabre hue of purple in the brake light's red glow. Gingerly she moved the edges of the baby blanket. Dead blue eyes looked up at her. "Oh, jeez. It's a kid."

Chapter Seven

A kid? He'd hit a kid? No, that was impossible. How would a kid get onto the property? The locked gate. The high walls. The all-seeing cameras. Chomp, who patrolled the grounds.

For an instant, the cold night air seemed to gel the blood in his veins, rousing all his sleeping fears. He was six, paralyzed and staring at those dead blue eyes.

Frozen in time, they triggered a howl inside him.

Valentina, her pale face hanging over dark shoulders. Blood pouring down her face, into her moonlight hair, dripping onto the floor. Her arms, poking out of the blue blanket, reaching for him, then limp and loose against her captor's back. And her eyes, half-closed, dead, staring after him, pleading, accusing.

Then the silence, oh, the silence. That silence would haunt him until the day he died.

He scrubbed a hand over his face, rubbing out that long-ago horror and bringing this night back into focus. The eyes. They weren't right. Dead, yes, but one-dimensional. The panic receded, leaving the jittery remnants of adrenaline shaking through his system.

He handed his cell phone to Valerie. "Call 911."

Crouching by the broken body, he took in the scene analytically. Not a child's eyes. A dummy's. Closer inspection revealed a child-size mannequin—the kind used in mall department stores. One someone had dressed in pink flannel pajamas with wooly lambs and fuzzy pink socks—like Valentina's on the night she disappeared.

Who had done this? And why? What in hell had they hoped to gain by the stunt?

"When the cops get here, tell them what happened." Without waiting for an answer, Nick took off into the woods in the direction from which someone had thrown the dummy into his car's path. The intruder would be long gone, but Nick had to do something. He couldn't just stay there and watch and wait.

"Where are you going?" Valerie called after him. But he didn't answer. The ache inside him went on and on and he needed to race ahead of the remembered weakness that had cost him his best friend. He needed to find the culprit who'd preyed on that weakness and pin him down. He needed answers.

His eyes adjusted to the deepening darkness and he plunged into the shadows of the woods. His dress shoes slipped on the rotting leaves. Branches caught on his jacket, dead fingers trying to hold him back. He didn't know where he was going, what path he was following, but he let the crawl of evil guide him.

Body running with sweat, he pushed himself harder, faster. Just as he had since the day he'd decided he'd never let weakness best him again. He'd thrown himself into lifting weights, learning self-defense, building his endurance. Soccer provided him with a way to hone mental and physical strategies. School became a proving ground for his mind until numbers, money and business no longer held any secrets.

He was strong, sharp, fast.

He would never again be helpless.

When he realized where his blind run was taking him, clammy dizziness fogged his brain. The pond. Through the trees, moonlight silvered the water, roped the ripples in black, making the surface appear to have swallowed a giant beast. His foot caught on something soft like flesh.

As he stumbled, he flung out an arm and stayed his fall against a tree trunk, but not before he smacked one knee into its ragged bark. Pain pulsing into his kneecap, he forced himself to turn around and look at the cause of his trip.

His chest cracked and seemed to open as if cleaved by an ax, leaving him raw and exposed. A small bubble of sound, half cry, half howl tore out of him.

Valentina.

No, no body. They'd never found her body.

But there, on the exact spot where the police had found the blanket soaked with Valentina's blood, lay Chomp's still body.

Nick's knee buckled as he tried to crouch, and he plopped on the ground beside Chomp. He cradled the Doberman in his lap. The slow beat of the dog's heart bumped against his thigh, and Nick mopped a hand over his face as relief sagged through him. "It's okay, Chomp. You'll be okay."

The night shook with wind, muttering through the naked tree limbs like witches conjuring a spell.

"Do you think there are witches in the woods, Nick?"

"Can't you hear them? Listen. They love to eat little girls."

"What about boys?"

"Well, girls are made of sugar and spice and everything nice."

"But witches like snails and puppy dog tails. Everybody knows that."

A branch broke nearby, the crack of it like the clash of blades in a duel. Cautious steps approached, then a dark form hovered close, uncertain.

"Nick?" Valerie asked. She sucked in a breath when she noticed the dog in his lap. Her hands clamped the shirt around her heart. "Oh, no, he's not...dead...is he?"

A cold waft, like a ghost, passed through his center. Echoes of Valentina existed in Valerie's countless quirks of posture and movement, and he hated her for stirring all the feelings he'd worked so hard to bury. Words caught in his throat and finally climbed their way up the pinched ladder of his throat. "He's alive. He needs a vet."

"The cops are here. They want to talk to you."

"We'd better get back then."

He rose, hefting the dog in his arms and his bruised left knee threatened to give again.

Valerie grabbed his elbow to steady him and her touch sparked with static. "Are you okay?"

"I cracked my knee on a tree." Seeking to lighten the loaded night, he let out a rough bark of laughter. "That's what I get for running through the woods in dress shoes instead of soccer cleats."

"Soccer, huh? Must be how you stay in such good shape."

That she'd noticed shouldn't warm him. It shouldn't matter. But it did. He limped his way through the familiar path around the pond toward the back entrance of the house. How many times had Valentina trailed him like that, full of questions and endless chatter. "You made good time out here."

"I run every day."

"You don't look like the runner type."

"Oh, yeah? And what's that?"

He ignored her question, needing to keep her talking to anchor his thoughts in the present. "Why running? I imagine you in ballet classes."

Her shrug hitched along his arm, and he sidestepped to inch more room between them. "When I was a teenager, running was the only acceptable excuse to leave home for half an hour without some sort of chaperone hanging around. Even then, I had to leave behind the precise course I'd take."

"Your parents were strict?"

She snorted. "A Navy commander at the height of maneuvers has nothing on my mother."

Beside him, her blue eyes were alive with a dynamic energy that connected with a vital part of him and somehow made his darkest emotions melt away.

Chomp whined and Valerie reached for his paw and rubbed it. "Why would anyone hurt an innocent dog?"

Nick climbed up the bluestone stairs that curved to the back patio, his knee screaming with pain with each step. "He got in the way."

"But he's just a dog."

"The anniversary. It brings out all the crazies." Only one person could know all the details that someone had so carefully reconstructed tonight.

Whoever had taken Valentina was back.

Was he working alone or had he trained a surrogate Valentina to bring the past alive? What did he want from reopening old wounds?

Chomp's labored breathing rasped in Nick's ear, and the need for violence exploded once again in his blood. He could not let hate win. The time had come to let out all the secrets, to expose the lies. To trap a kidnapper.

"I'll do your interview instead of Rita," Nick said at the top of the stone stairs.

Valerie's step faltered. "There's no point if you're only going to dance around the issue. Protecting Valentina's privacy seems to be a hot button for you."

"Telling Valentina's story means a lot to Rita."

Valerie tilted her head as if he'd revealed a secret. "You love her."

"She's been good to me." Once someone made a mistake, could any amount of compensation erase it? Even if his financial skill earned Rita all the riches in the world, it would never make up for losing Valentina. "I owe her."

"I BELIEVE RITA HAS legionellosis," Dr. Marzan said, and stuffed the stethoscope back into his black bag.

His bald head shone under the room's ambient light. Though easily in his seventies, with his fit body and lightly lined face, he could pass for a man twenty years younger. He was a dying breed. Nick didn't know of any other doctor in the area who still made house calls or who truly seemed to care about his patients' wellness. He'd shown up for a follow-up visit after the cops were done with taking Nick's, Valerie's and Mike's statements and after they'd all picked at the dinner Holly had prepared.

"Legionnaires' Disease?" Nick frowned. "Where would she have picked it up?"

"A place with mold—like a malfunctioning air-conditioning system or a hot tub."

Nick had looked up Rita's itinerary. She'd stayed at an older hotel in Chicago because the convention hotel was full. "A hotel?"

Dr. Marzan nodded and made a noise that sounded like a yes. "Outbreaks tend to happen in summer and early fall. I'll need to do a chest X-ray and run other lab tests to be sure."

"I'll bring her in first thing in the morning."

"Don't speak as if…I'm not here," Rita said weakly. Her eyes fought to stay open.

Nick sat at the edge of the bed. "I thought you'd fallen asleep."

Rita reached a hand toward him, and he held the fragile bones in his palm. "I'll go if Valentina comes with me."

Dr. Marzan shot Nick a questioning look that Nick ignored. Valerie again. Everything that had happened in the last few days seemed to revolve around her. How little it had taken for her to insert herself in Rita's life. Why wasn't Joe picking up anything off-color in her background?

"Then she'll go with you." Not that Nick had a choice in the matter. Not if he wanted to keep the situation under control. "Rest now."

"You'll see, Nicolas. I'm right."

Nick banked his sudden annoyance at Valerie's interference, and followed Dr. Marzan out into the sharp bite of night. To unearth Valerie's plans, he needed to keep his personal feelings out of play and stay objective. Rita was counting on him to keep her safe. "How bad is this disease?"

The doctor pushed his rimless glasses up his nose. "It affects primarily the lungs. Because of her age, and her weakened immune system from her kidney infection over the summer, she's more susceptible to complications. If she puts off care too long, it can lead to chronic lung disease. With prompt care, it usually clears up in a few weeks."

"She'll be there tomorrow, then. And if she needs hospitalization, I expect you to admit her."

Dr. Marzan nodded. "Bring her round the hospital at nine. I'll make sure everything is ready for her."

As Dr. Marzan drove away in his beat-up Volvo, Nick spotted the extra patrol the police department had promised cruising by the front gates. With Chomp recovering at the animal hospital, Nick would have to beef up the security system.

Poisoning, the vet had said, from tainted meat. Which

only stirred up Nick's suspicions because Chomp had been trained to accept food from only two people—Lionel and Holly. And Nick trusted both of them with his life.

MIND PREOCCUPIED, Nick marched up the front steps and practically ran into a distracted Evan Gardner as he plowed out the door.

"I have to bring in more equipment," Gardner said. His bushy eyebrows met at the center of his pleated forehead. "Do you mind?"

Gardner didn't wait for an answer, but continued down the stairs to his truck. Nick reversed his path and followed him. Cold wind moaned through the trees and spiked right through the weave of his shirt. "What kind of equipment?"

"An ELF meter for one. And an audio enhancer."

"ELF meter?" This was scientific?

Gardner riffled through the stacks of gear under the cap over the truck bed. "Extremely low frequency. The meter measures sound waves that the human ear can't hear." He pulled out a black handheld device. "Ah, here it is."

"How did you meet Rita?" Nick leaned against the truck—as much to keep out of the wind's way as to appear relaxed.

Gardner stuffed the meter in the pocket of his tweed jacket, then kept rummaging through his gear. "I met her ten days ago in Chicago. After my panel at the convention, she arranged to meet me for dinner at her hotel."

"What convinced you to trek all this way?"

Gardner's eyebrows rose and his face became animated. "Most of the paranormal activity I've had the opportunity to research has been apparitions. This was a chance to study an auditory event."

"Did you hear the cries last night?" As if he'd say he hadn't.

Gardner made an aha sound, then pulled out a laptop. "Yes, but I don't think there's a paranormal event going on in the tower room."

"No?" Nick said, surprised.

"I think it's physical."

"What makes you think that?"

Gardner fired up the computer, checked on the battery's status and pulled out a power cord. "Even though the physical structure is destroyed, the energy structure can stay behind. I didn't pick up anything on the digital or video cameras. No orbs, no mists, no apparitions. Nothing on the night-vision scope. The EMF—electromagnetic field—meter showed no pools of excessive energy. No cold spots registered on the thermometer. And there were no anomalies on the compass. The only piece of equipment to pick up anything was the tape recorder."

Gardner put aside the laptop and handed Nick his battered logbook. As if all that gobbledygook and chicken scratch handwriting meant anything to him. How in the world was all that supposed to prove that a ghost existed or didn't exist? "Then what causes the cries?"

Gardner took back his log and plopped the laptop in Nick's hands. "Infrasound. Like that caused by background radiation from microwave ovens or overhead power lines."

"Sounds like more bull."

Gardner shot him a scathing look. "Sometimes sound waves can make it appear as if there's an otherworldly phenomenon going on, when it's just pulses below our hearing range vibrating something in the room."

Nick grumbled unconvinced.

"Infrasound can also cause vision irregularities, blurring or vibrating the visual field. The eyeball has a resonant frequency of nineteen hertz, so if you're standing some place that's vibrating at nineteen hertz, your eyeball will vibrate along with the wave."

"So someone could think they saw something, but it's really just their eyeball vibrating?"

Gardner's smile widened like a barn door as if pleased that Nick finally understood. "Exactly."

Gardner shut the truck's back gate and started toward the house, various cords sticking out from under one arm. "Peripheral vision is extremely sensitive to movement and could make the vibration seem like a blurry gray ghost. Infrasonic waves also trigger the fight-or-flight response, which explains why some people feel cold or the backs of their necks tingling or a strange feeling in their stomachs in the presence of a so-called ghost."

"I'm still not getting how that makes a baby cry."

Gardner bent down and tapped the house's foundation with the knuckles of one hand. "Old buildings have thicker walls that resonate better."

"That's supposed to convince me?" Nick asked.

Gardner whirled to face him and shook a finger in Nick's face. "Just because I'm studying extraordinary activity doesn't mean I abandon ordinary logic. In order to define a fact, I assume as little as possible and consider all angles. I'll need to set up some measuring equipment in the cellar. And really, if you think about it, everything we know about our world was at one time unknown."

Would Gardner now find an expensive "treatment" to rid the mansion of those infrasound waves?

If Gardner was trying to convince Rita that she had a ghost haunting the tower room, he certainly wasn't going about it in a very convincing way. On the other hand, if he was in cahoots with Valerie to extort money from Rita, then convincing Rita that Valentina's ghost wasn't haunting the tower room and, therefore, Valentina was still alive, ta-da, in the form of Valerie, then his gizmos and gadgets and his fancy explanations were going to go a long way to prove that point. A point Rita was already sure was true. But having Gardner stick around a bit longer also gave Nick a chance to debunk the fraud.

"Go ahead, set up what you need." Nick handed Gardner his laptop. "But don't bother Ms. Meadows with any of your findings. She's too ill."

Gardner and his equipment started for the basement. After a few steps, he stopped. "I'm not doing this for the money, you know."

"Then why?"

"For data. For science. For understanding."

And Gardner's unblinking expression gave Nick the impression Gardner really believed the crap he was trying to feed Nick.

But then, confidence was a con man's best asset.

Chapter Eight

The nausea started soon after Valerie reached her room.
The hot shower did nothing to help the mad churning
of her stomach. Neither did the Pepto-Bismol tablets
she'd chewed. She blamed the greasy food from lunch
and the stress of the day. She should have skipped
dinner, but hadn't wanted to get on Holly's bad side any
more than she already was. She'd forced down the
heavy chowder, the overcooked lemon sole and the
bitter steamed broccoli.

Sitting on the bed, shivering in her fleece hoodie and
sweatpants, she finally managed to reach Higgins on his
cell.

"What's up, kiddo? Tell me you're on schedule."

Valerie reached for the blue-and-white afghan at the
foot of the bed and pulled it over her legs. "About that…
I got the interview with Kirby Cicco taped. I'm trying to
arrange one with a chauffeur who was on the suspect list
and another with the widow of the landscaper who sup-
posedly made a deathbed confession to the kidnapping.
For some reason, no one ever took his admission of guilt

seriously. But Ms. Meadows fell ill, so I'll have to reschedule her interview. I'm going to have to stay over the weekend."

"All you have is one interview?"

Valerie tucked a loose strand of hair behind her ear. With Higgins it was better to keep pointing out the positive. "There are some new developments."

"Such as?"

She shook away the image of the dummy's body flying into the path of Nick's car. "Someone is setting up a scenario ripe for blackmail."

"How so?"

"Someone broke into the mansion and left behind a necklace that belonged to Valentina and a note saying they knew where she was. Nobody will confirm this, but I have a feeling Valentina was wearing the necklace the night she disappeared.

"Then on our way back from the prison interview, someone threw a child-size mannequin in front of the car. It was dressed like Valentina on the night she disappeared. I think the kidnapper's back, and he wants the ransom he was cheated out of twenty-five years ago when a random patrol car messed up the exchange."

The rubber band give-and-take of highway traffic whooshed in the background. "Why wait that long?"

"That's what I need to figure out."

"You're a coordinator, not a reporter."

Valerie leaned forward and hugged her knees with her free arm, hoping to calm the greasy eels of nausea snaking through her stomach. "But just think, if you could air a resolution to the Meadows's kidnapping, you'd have Mr. Meadows's undying gratitude. Not to mention the ratings."

"What makes you think you can solve this mystery when no one else has been able to in twenty-five years?"

A gut feeling. But that wouldn't fly with Higgins. He wanted facts. So she swallowed down a wave of sickness souring her throat and gave him a half lie. "I've found someone who was there the night of the kidnapping."

"Sounds like tired territory."

How old had Nick been at the time of the kidnapping? Five? Six? Given his history with Moongate, he would have been at the party. How much had he seen? "He's never told his story to anyone before."

"But he told you?" Higgins pushed.

Not yet. "Yes."

"Get it on tape."

She lay down on her side, curled up in a fetal position, but the queasiness didn't ebb. Nick had agreed to the interview, but she wasn't convinced he'd tell her his deep, dark secrets. Building trust would take more than a day. "It's going to take some time."

"Well, kiddo, time's one thing you don't have much of. The segment airs in five days. If it doesn't, you're out of a job."

Because Mr. Meadows would not be pleased, and Higgins had a habit of taking out Mr. Meadows's wrath on his underlings. "I can solve this."

"Your job isn't to solve the case. Your job is to get the package ready."

Valerie pushed harder. "Think eternal gratitude. Think skyrocketing ratings when you scoop everyone else."

"Hmm…" Higgins paused.

Valerie pressed a hand to her heaving stomach as Higgins drew up a mental pros-and-cons list.

"Don't get yourself in trouble, kiddo," he said. "I'm not going to bail you out."

The possible ratings won out. Valerie attempted a smile, but the pull of muscles seemed to invite her stomach's contents to climb up her throat. "Thanks. I won't."

"Keep me up-to-date."

She hung up and barely made it in time to the bathroom before she was violently sick.

VALERIE AWOKE WITH A START, dazed and disoriented, her heart in her throat, darkness choking her.

Where was she? What day was this?

The sounds were distant, the colors faded, but the terror and the confusion remained brightly etched. Anguish lingered, thick and heavy, and the dry salt of her tears caked her cheeks.

Pushing her hair off her face, she breathed in deeply. Moongate. Thursday—no, Friday by now. She was on assignment, not caught in the sticky web of her nightmare. She was okay.

With a flick of her wrist, she pulled away the twist of sheets and blankets and sat on the edge of the bed, hands planted firmly at her sides to steady the dizziness bouncing the room around.

The dream was old, recurrent. As always, it dogged her

into sleep on the heels of stress. And yesterday had been chock-full of stress between the interview, the dummycide and the stomach bug.

And Nick.

Like a fingerprint on her psyche, she'd been aware of him every minute of the interview, of the ride home, of that mad race into those dark woods. The space he'd occupied. The rhythm of his every breath. The chaos of his thoughts. And that awareness had tampered with her usual focus. She'd wanted to go to him and reassure him.

As if he needed any reassuring. The man was an island. He needed no one—least of all her.

She dreaded looking at the interview tape. What if she'd messed up because of her distraction? What if all she'd managed to get out of Kirby Cicco was crap?

Worrying before she had the facts was useless. Obsessing over Nick and the strange pull he had on her wasn't going to help her, either.

She clicked on the bedside lamp, making the darkness retreat. Hugging her knees, she plucked at the remnants of the dream and tried to label the shadows that still trembled inside her. Something, like a word on the tip of the tongue that the brain couldn't quite retrieve, scratched at her, begging her to remember.

A soft cry rode in through the chilly night air. She cocked her head and tuned into it. A baby's cry. The sad sobs echoed inside her chest, and she spread a palm over her throat as if to hold them in. Helpless whimpers, like a child resigning itself to a fate of abandonment.

Rita's ghost child? Valentina?

Still shaky from her bout of stomach sourness, Valerie wrapped an afghan around her shoulders and followed the sounds of the cries down the hallway and up the narrow stairs to the tower room.

As she neared the door, the tormented screams wailed from inside the empty room. She reached for the latch, hesitated. "Stop it. There's no baby. Ghosts don't exist."

With a determined push, she pressed the iron plunger. The door opened, whispering like frenzied termites across the wood floor, and the cries instantly ceased.

Valerie stepped into the room and stopped in a ray of moonlight drawing a rectangle on the wide pine planks. Through the uncurtained windows, Mount Monadnock loomed black against the dark slate of the sky. Tree limbs sketched an intricate web of shadows across the lawn. The light reflecting off the pond's surface gleamed like white blood on black veins.

The walls around her shimmered and shifted. She swiveled her head, searching—for what? Valerie's hands clamped over her still-sore stomach. Something was wrong. The bed, the storage chest, the rug were all where they'd been when Nick had given her a tour of the mansion, but two blanket tents squirmed on the tic-tac-toe area rug, the beam of the flashlight between them bouncing around the room like a searchlight.

As if someone had flicked on an old movie projector, a grainy film rolled through her head and into the room.

"Go fish!"
The blue lump moved, reaching for a card.

A girlish giggle exploded from the pink lump. "I win! I win!"

"No fair! You cheated."

"You can't cheat at Go Fish, Nick."

A deck of cards came spewing out from the opening between the tents. "I'm leaving."

Nick scrambled to his feet, but with a tug of both hands, Valentina pulled him back down. "No, Nick, stay! Tell me a story."

"I don't know any more stories." A grumpy Nick fished a Matchbox race car from each pocket of his jeans.

"Read me a book." Flinging the blanket behind her like a cape, Valentina raced to the built-in shelves next to her pink-canopied bed and picked out an armful of Dr. Seuss books. She dumped them in Nick's lap. He yelped, tossing them aside. "Hey, careful!"

Valentina reached into the fan of books for *Green Eggs and Ham*. "Start with this one."

Nick flung the book away. "I'm not good at reading."

Valentina rescued the tome. "Are, too. And your mom said you have to watch me."

Reluctantly, Nick spread the book across his lap and read haltingly, but Valentina didn't seem to notice. Thumb in her mouth, she nestled her head into his shoulder with a satisfied sigh and her lashes soon fluttered shut. He covered her with his blanket, then curled up next to her—a yang to her yin—and puttered with the race cars. Minutes later, he tugged absently at the loose blanket beside him, pulled it over his head and soon fell asleep, a car in each hand, the discarded book pillowing his head. The forgotten flashlight rolled across the floor and under the bed.

A blurry form stretched across the floor, shadowing the moonlit lumps of the sleeping children, watching. A strong whiff of something sour peeled off the shadow-skewed figure.

She opened her eyes, blinked and, through the hood of the blanket, searched the monster's face leaning over her. Tremors rattled through her flesh, numbing her arms and legs. Her clear blue eyes widened, widened. Her mouth opened.

"Wake up, Nick! Wake up!" she wanted to scream, but the words clogged in her dry throat.

Then two black hands came toward her....

A hand clamped around Valerie's shoulder and she screamed.

ALTHOUGH HE'D HIRED a nurse to watch over Rita, and although his mother slept nearby, Nick wanted to stick around the mansion in case Rita's health took a turn for the worse during the night.

He settled in Rita's office and went through the pile of papers on her desk, making short work of the business end of things. The invitations to holiday parties—who sent out Christmas party invitations in October?—he left for her until she got better. And she would get better. No bacteria was going to get the best of her when the kidnapping of her child and the death of her husband—the virtual falling apart of her whole world—hadn't. She was too strong.

Joe called around ten with an update.

"Simon Higgins is up to his eyeballs in debt after a dubious investment backfired," Joe said. "Gossip around the station has it that that's why he's so cozy with Bailey Bergeron, a debutante with a hefty trust fund, playing at the working girl game."

"You think he's after her money?"

"That's the rumor. From what I gather, Higgins is in tight with Mr. Meadows, too. Cigar and whiskey buddies. Weekends on the yacht type thing. Close enough to find out family secrets the rest of the world might not know."

That gave Higgins a handy way of getting all the details correct—the necklace, the dummy's clothes, the dog left under just the right tree.

"If Higgins already has his hands on a means to clear his debt with the deb, why bother with the Valentina charade?"

"He's ambitious. The station's ratings have gone down in their market share. Maybe he wants something to raise the ratings. Sweeps are coming. Edmund Meadows is old. He doesn't have any heirs, except for his niece, Rita. Maybe Higgins figures there's room for him to move up to being the big boss."

"Not when he's that far in debt." Valerie was ambitious, too. Had Higgins promised her a promotion to meatier stories in exchange for her cooperation? Was Higgins hoping "finding" Valentina would gain him enough cash to buy himself a chunk of the station should Edmund die or decide to sell and retire?

"I'm going to keep digging," Joe said.

"Have you found Gordon Archer yet?" Nick stood, unable to take the confines of the chair. Outside the criss-cross of shadows on the lawn formed jagged prison bars.

"He's had three addresses since his stay as a guest of the Florida state prison system last year," Joe said. "Seems he's left a trail of complaints behind each. He's between addresses right now."

No surprise. For some people, there was no rehabilita-tion. Just as a leopard couldn't change its spots, a man like Gordon rarely changed his modus operandi. What was he building up to with these small cons? Payback?

"But I hit the jackpot." Joe clicked his pen in a victorious cheer. "Archer bought a first-class airline ticket from Miami to Manchester. He arrived in New Hampshire two days ago."

Same as Valerie. Was there a connection? "Then you need to get back here."

"You want me to drop the leads I have on Evan Gardner and Valerie Zea?"

Nick let out a long breath. "What did you find?"

"I've gotten my hands on past grant applications made by Dr. Gardner. It seems he doesn't care who butters his bread. He's accepted money from skeptic organizations as well as from organizations that seek to promote the paranormal."

Nick couldn't decide if that made Gardner more or less suspicious. What would he agree to do to further his quest for data, science and understanding? "What about Valerie Zea?"

"I've got a feeling. I'm heading to the courthouse tomorrow to check into something."

"Get back as soon as you can. Any word from your lab guy?"

"He can get DNA off the cup you sent. It's going to take a couple more days to get results."

"I'll pay a premium to expedite."

"I'll let him know."

Joe's report had added more questions, but provided no answers. Holding down the fort and seeing that no harm came to Rita was still up to Nick.

Just as he plugged in his laptop, the phantom baby's cries arose like mist out of the night. The disquieting warble sounded much too close to the baleful howl that keened inside him. Elbows on the desk, he rested his head in his palms and wished the damning cries away.

What if ghosts did exist? What if it was Valentina crying every night because he'd failed her when he was the only one who could have saved her?

He yanked off his tie and hurled it across the desk. What could a skinny, sickly six-year-old have done to stop the black, hulking monster who'd swept his friend away?

Nick shoved the chair back and paced the room.

You could've cried. You could've yelled. You could've run for help.

He growled his frustration, then tilted his head back to stare at the ceiling.

The only reason the cries wailed tonight was because Gardner had needed the door closed, needed to conjure up the tormenting sounds to measure them and find their root source.

Nick went back to the desk, tried to concentrate on the analysis he needed to finish for his rescheduled meeting with Emma Hanley and Carter Stokke tomorrow, but the numbers blurred on the screen. "Take a break. Shake it off."

He might as well head up to the tower room and check on Gardner's "scientific" methods and make sure the root cause wasn't going to entail an expensive purge.

As he climbed the tower staircase, the cries stopped. And when he got to the tower room, it wasn't the sight of Gardner busy twisting dials and adjusting gizmos that met him. It was Valerie, wandering around the room looking like a ghost in her pale pink flannel pajamas and bare feet, her flaxen hair gleaming like liquid platinum in the moonlight. And with that blanket thrown over her shoulders, for an instant, he was assaulted with a powerful punch of déjà vu.

Nick didn't drink. Not for any altruistic reasons, but because his father had come up with his craziest ideas under the influence of alcohol. Just watching him, beer in hand, spin his schemes had thrown Nick into an out-of-control reel that made him puke half his meals, keeping him small and weak for his age. And right now, looking at Valerie, that drunk, spun-out sensation prickled through his senses in an acute kind of pain.

The expression on Valerie's face, her moonlight-silvered eyes, the way she chewed on her thumbnail transposed themselves onto the faded photographs he carried inside his heart. A tug of memory pulled him into the room. Then an infinite pang of loss stopped him cold.

She'd never been here. She couldn't know.

Then like his father when a scheme boomeranged, he exploded.

He clamped a hand around Valerie's shoulder. She screamed.

He twisted her around to face him. "What kind of sick game are you playing?"

At the sight of her ashen, petrified face his hand vaulted off her shoulder. What the hell was wrong with him? He was *not* his father. He was better than that.

"You were there," she breathed, eyes bright moonstones in the room's thin light. "That night. You were right there on that rug with Valentina."

His first instinct was to deny, to defend the scared six-year-old, to move as far away from her as he could. Instead he shifted to trap her body between his and the wall.

She wrung two handfuls of his shirt. The blue blanket dropped from her shoulders and pooled at their feet. "What really happened to Valentina?"

His voice sounded odd and hollow, even to him. "You've done your research. You tell me."

"The research isn't accurate. You should know."

"I was six. I don't remember anything."

"Playing Go Fish with Valentina, reading her *Green Eggs and Ham*. You both fell asleep on the floor. The research—*every single account*—said she was taken from her bed."

He'd seen things. Seen how cruel people could be, and he hadn't been able to stop the pain. Every time his father had locked the bedroom door. Every time he'd heard his mother beg. Every time he'd looked at her bruises. He'd felt helpless.

Until Valentina.

After Rita had taken him and Holly in, three-year-old Valentina had followed him around the mansion like a puppy. At first, he'd resented her clinginess. But soon he'd fallen for the innocent adoration in her big, blue eyes. Even if he hadn't deserved it, her childish hero worship had made him feel strong, wanted—needed.

He wasn't going to think about the feelings Valerie was trying to stir; he simply refused to get lost that far inside his own head. "That's a pretty fantasy you're spinning. How can all those accounts be wrong?"

Her forehead rucked, then her gaze strayed to the tic-tac-toe rug, and she shuddered. "I—I sense it."

"So you're psychic now?"

That seemed to knock her out of her trance. Her hands let go of his shirt. She gave a short, rough laugh. "I wish."

He took a step toward her, slid a hand up into the soft fall of her hair to prove to himself that it wasn't as soft as Valentina's. He leaned in, mouth hovering close to her ear.

"According to Gardner, there is no paranormal happening here," Nick whispered. "No orbs, no mists, no apparitions. Seeing ghosts doesn't wash, *Val*."

"The cries."

Because the moonlight spotlighted her lips, because he couldn't help the mad urge to sample them, he brought his mouth to hers. The jolt was a spike of lightning that bolted straight into his gut. The taste of her so warm, so rich, so impossibly contenting, rushed to his head, leaving him light-headed and longing for more. "Infrasound."

Her breath puffed against his cheek. "I heard them."

The sweet-and-spicy ginger of her scent wound around his senses, and he hoped to God the hum of satisfaction vibrating against his throat came from her and not him. "Who told you this pretty story, Val?"

"Nobody." With a helpless moan, she looped her hands behind his neck. Her lips skimmed the skin of his neck, de-railing his logic. "You were there, Nick. What did you see?"

Fighting for control, his muscles bunched, readying to flee from this unexpected onslaught. Staying the course, tasting her as if she had no effect on him, took all of his will, yet none of it. Her body pliantly yielded to his, her small hands pulled him closer, her heat melded into him. She was the strongest of drinks, the most potent of drugs, the most addictive of substances. His blood boiled with need. His mind turned into a complete and mindless blank.

"Blood," Nick rasped in her ear. His fingers tightened in her hair. "Lots of blood."

She rubbed her cheek against his. Soft, so soft. "What else?"

"Dead eyes." He tasted the rapid pulse at the base of her neck, drank in the strong beat of its life force.

She sucked in a long, shaky breath. "What else, Nick?"

He kissed her for a long count of ten, while an internal war burned with fervor. *She is not getting to me. I am in control.* "A black monster. Is that what you want to hear, Val?"

Her fingers skimmed his temples. Her gaze, wide and aware, bored into his as if she felt his pain, understood it. "Tell me about the monster."

Purge yourself, the siren song of relief called to him.

"He was dressed in black." Nick's arms tightened around her waist, her shoulders, pressing her closer as if he needed her solid presence to hold him up. "He wore a ski mask over his face."

He erased the bitter memory of terror with the tang of her tongue. The taste of her clung to him, marked him. And when he pulled away, sweet satisfaction thrummed through him at the sight of her dazed eyes, her unsteady stance and the finger pressed against her lips as if to hold in his kiss. That small unconscious gesture sent his blood churning again. "She's dead, Val. Valentina is dead. You're right. I was there. I saw the blood. I saw the dead eyes. And every piece of evidence I've collected since then says that she's dead."

Valerie reached a hand out to him, but he stepped back. He'd made a mistake. He'd given her too much, given her a new avenue to exploit. Another weakness. He couldn't afford to let her touch him. Not when his balance was so precariously on edge. Not when all he wanted was to taste her again, take her, possess her. "Who are you working with? What do you want from us?"

Baffled, she shook her head. "No, Nick, no."

Controlling Valerie's playing of Valentina to save Rita was one thing. Having himself fall for an imposter was quite another.

But he was. As impossible as it was, he was falling for

her. For the moonlit innocence, the soothing balm of her touch, the electric fire of her kiss. And he could not let her see the hold she'd gained.

The sound of his voice reported around the hexagonal room like a hail of gunfire. "Then tell me how you know about the cards and the books."

A needle of guilt stabbed him when she flinched. But before he could press his advantage, a flash outside caught his attention.

"What the—"

He strode to the window. Through the lattice of frost, a phosphorescent figure floated like a ghost across the lawn and into the woods.

Chapter Nine

Like the unfortunate Alice of Wonderland fame, in the moonlit tower room, Valerie fell into some sort of alternate universe that fogged her mind and turned her world upside down with Nick as her balancing center.

The intensity of his eyes tugged at her with a pull as inescapable as gravity. Something in them made Valerie want to delve deeper even though every instinct told her to look away before she got sucked into a place she couldn't escape.

As if he were purging himself, Nick plundered her mouth once again. Wow, the guy could certainly kiss. This intimate connection reached across time and warmed the cold darkness that sealed her heart. She sighed into him, letting go of all the fears that knotted her mind and body after the disturbing viewing of the long-ago film of Nick and Valentina.

For a brief moment, secure in his arms, she no longer needed to search. She had found. She was home. Then just as quickly, doubt caught up to her. How could this man she'd never met until two days ago be the one to anchor her into herself?

The answer couldn't be that simple.

The answer couldn't be him.

As if to prove her right, Nick moved away. She pressed a finger against her lips, desperately trying to hold on to the fleeting sense of wholeness she'd felt in his arms.

"She's dead, Val." Nick's voice sliced knife-sharp into the night. "Valentina is dead. You're right. I was there. I saw the blood. I saw the dead eyes. And every piece of evidence I've collected since then says that she's dead."

Heart aching for him, she reached out and found only empty air.

"Who are you working with? What do you want from us?"

"No, Nick, no." She shook her head. He was asking questions meant to paint her guilty of a crime she hadn't committed. In his eyes, she was a fraud, but in hers, he was suddenly the key to the truth. She needed to make him believe she wasn't out to hurt the Meadows family, but simply to find answers.

His voice continued to batter against her brain. The words made no sense.

"What the—" He rushed by her.

"Nick?" The room was spinning and she flattened her palms against the wall to hold herself up.

"Go back to your room," he said.

She bolted off the wall. "What? No. We need to talk."

He tore down the tower stairs two at a time. She ran after him, glad the movement finally broke through the disorienting fog in her mind. "Where are you going?"

"We have a damned ghost hunter in the house. Let

Gardner go chase after apparitions." Nick charged down the hall as if rocket-propelled and pounded through the kitchen door. His bruised knee finally caught up to him and made him limp across the checkerboard tiles.

"What are you talking about?" Valerie asked.

Nick flipped on the lights. The stark fluorescence bounced off every gleaming stainless steel surface and glossy granite counter in a blinding way. "Didn't you see that *thing* outside?"

She'd been too lost in Nick's kiss to notice much of anything. "What thing?"

Nick didn't answer, but rummaged through a drawer filled with odds and ends.

"We'll talk in the morning," Nick said, dismissing her.

"Is that a request or a command?"

"Which is more likely to get me your cooperation?"

"Since you're asking so nicely. Neither. I'll stick around for the ghost hunt."

Nick found a flashlight and tested it, then started down a flight of stairs that led into the basement. Pale light eked from the bottom of the gray steps. "Gardner!"

No answer floated up.

"Gardner! Where the hell are you?" Nick asked as he reached the basement and flashed his light around.

The basement was a dark crypt that twisted along the house's puzzle-piece floor plan. The earthen floor was cold against Valerie's bare feet and powdery dirt oozed between her toes. The thick air pressed against her lungs. She didn't do dark and claustrophobic very well. Maybe she should have done the logical thing and gone back to her room, but there were too many unanswered questions. And the part of her that needed to know won over the chicken side that wanted to hide.

The shadows from the widely separated bulbs, swinging on electrical cords, gave the space a sinister feel as if eyes were everywhere, watching, waiting, threatening. Instinctively, she reached for Nick's shirt and hung on as he hunched over and swept his flashlight into the dark recesses the weak bulbs didn't reach. Copper pipes caked with green crud snaked and angled along the low ceiling. No wonder the water tasted funny. Drapes of cobwebs hung from the rafters and air ducts, making her miss the afghan she'd forgotten in the tower room.

"What makes you think Dr. Gardner is down here?" she asked.

"He's measuring. Something about low frequency waves."

Once they passed the cellar hatch that provided access to the outside, the air throbbed with groans from the ancient furnace firing heat from a dark corner, and from moans emanating from Evan Gardner's body, splattered across the breadth of his equipment.

Valerie rushed by Nick and knelt beside the professor, feeling for broken bones. Blood glistened darkly against his dirty-blond hair. "Dr. Gardner? Evan? Are you okay?"

Hand to his temple, he rolled over. "Someone hit me from behind."

He tried to sit up, but Valerie held him back. "I don't think you should move."

"I'm okay," Evan insisted and sat up. He pulled a handkerchief from the pocket of his jacket and patted it against the cut on his head. "Just a bit of ringing."

Nick pointed the beam of his flashlight at a rock the size of a fist, stained with fresh blood. "Looks like this was the weapon of choice."

"You need a doctor," Valerie said.

Evan shook his head and winced. "No time."

"You could have a concussion."

"I'm on to something." Evan crawled forward and reached for what was left of his laptop and moaned.

Nick's light sliced over the broken pieces of Evan's equipment.

Evan swore with a viciousness that made Valerie jump. "Would you look at this! Hitting me is one thing. But this—" He reached for the plastic pieces that once made up some sort of meter. "This is expensive equipment. If you don't want me here, just tell me to get out. Don't go around destroying my research."

"Trust me," Nick said. "I'd kick you out before I'd destroy your equipment. But Rita wants you here, so you get to stay—safe and sound."

Evan pressed at some keys on the laptop in his lap as if the action could bring the computer back to life. "I was just pinning down the source of the infrasound, when *pow*, my lights went out." He rifled through the mess of electronic pieces. "My data's gone."

"Are you sure?" Nick asked.

"Of course I'm sure."

"How important is this data to your finding the source of the cries?"

"It's *data*," Evan said, as if he'd lost his firstborn. Then he perked up. "At least I still have the recorder in the tower room."

Really? Valerie would have to retrieve the tape and see if it had captured the conversation she'd had with Nick. He'd been there the night of Valentina's kidnapping. He'd seen the kidnapper. And if the evidence of his admission was on tape, then he couldn't just brush her away when she pressed him for more details.

"Are you up to investigating a ghost?" Nick asked Evan. "Or do you need a trip to the emergency room?"

Evan raised an eyebrow and stuffed the bloody hand-kerchief back in his pocket. "A ghost?"

"I saw something green and phosphorescent glide across the lawn outside."

"Interesting. An orb? A mist?"

"More like a life-size blob."

Evan scrambled up to his feet, wobbled a little, then pointed toward the stairs. "I have more equipment in the truck."

Minutes later, hunched over like some caricature of Sherlock Holmes searching for a clue, Evan fanned Nick's flashlight across the lawn where Nick had spotted the ghost. Nick and Valerie trailed behind him.

The raw night air needled through Valerie's flannel pajamas, making her shiver. She clamped her teeth tight so Nick wouldn't hear them chatter and insist she go back to the house as he'd already attempted several times. There was no way she was missing the show. Not when she had a feeling it somehow connected with her story.

Evan stopped near the gazebo by the pond. "Not a ghost."

"What then?" Nick asked, clearly losing patience with Evan's paranormal sleuthing.

Evan poked his head in a bush and came out with a glowing green sheet. "Phosphorescent paint. Someone wanted you to think there was a ghost." He clucked. "Not very convincing, if you ask me."

"Can you tell where the paint came from?"

The gaudy house at the mouth of Windemere Drive came to Valerie's mind.

Evan handed Nick the sheet. "You want a crime lab, call *CSI*. I do ghosts, not silly Halloween jokes." He wiped traces of the glow-in-the-dark paint from his fingers with his bloodstained handkerchief. "If you'll excuse me. I need some aspirin, then I need to go see if I can recapture the data I've lost. It was just getting interesting."

First the dummy, then the dog, now this "ghost." They were more than mere jokes. They were a warning. Was it her fault because she'd insisted on pursuing the story? Was her curiosity putting Nick and Rita in danger?

"Evan, wait up!" Valerie shouted after the professor. She needed to get to that tape before he did and make a copy. Nick was the key. He'd seen Valentina's kidnapper. And just maybe more answers were buried in his subconscious. Someone wanted to keep Nick quiet, making the retrieval of those memories that much more important.

Shivering in the cold night air, she hesitated for a moment and looked at Nick over her shoulder. Too many ghosts traipsed after him, weighing him down. The last thing she'd wanted to do with this story was to hurt anyone. If she'd made things worse for Nick, she had to fix the situation. Maybe then she wouldn't feel so responsible for upsetting his world. He needed peace as much as Rita did. But that peace wouldn't come without answers. "I'll help you find Valentina."

Nick scoffed as he carefully folded the doctored sheet. "What can you do that I haven't already done at least twice?"

"I can listen. I can ask questions you might not have thought of. I can look at things from a different perspective."

"How do I know I'm not getting in bed with the enemy—so to speak?"

She cocked her head. "Then at least you know where she is and what she's up to."

He kept folding the sheet. "Go. I'll handle the police."

She didn't want to go, not when Nick seemed so glum and alone, but the sound of Evan's truck door creaking open resounded in the night. She had to go, now, before Evan went to the tower room and she'd lost her first concrete evidence that the film playing in her mind was real. "I'll talk to you in the morning."

While Evan rummaged in the back of his truck for equipment, Valerie rushed up the stairs to the tower room. She found the digital recorder by the door, its Bionic Ear audio enhancer poised to capture every sound in the room.

But the memory card inside the recorder was gone.

THE DISTRACTION had worked. It wouldn't fool them for long, but he'd gotten what he needed. She was getting too close to the truth. And the truth would upset too many lives. He had to keep them busy—chasing more phantoms—until he'd set his trap and gotten what was his.

The rest needed to stay buried.

He couldn't let anyone rush him. Not this time. All the details had to be right. And all he needed was a few more days.

"LIONEL'S GOING TO DRIVE—" Nick started to say as Valerie entered the dining room the next morning. She held up a hand, closed her eyes and shook her head. No matter how many times she'd rolled around what had happened last night in her mind, no answers had come. All she had to show for her efforts was sleep deprivation and a pounding headache.

"Coffee?" she croaked.

"Twenty degrees to your right, ten paces," Nick said, and she definitely detected a note of amusement in his voice.

Mike sniggered as he dug into a pile of scrambled eggs and English muffins spread thick with butter and blueberry jam. "Don't talk to her until she's downed her first cup or she'll bite your head off."

"Good to know."

"Are these the biggest cups you have?" Valerie yearned for her usual large take-out cup of French vanilla.

"I'm afraid so."

With a groan, she carefully measured a quarter inch of cream into one of the tiny cups next to the urn. Could they make them any smaller? She filled it to the brim with coffee and slammed the contents down in one gulp. She filled the cup again, drank, then sighed as the fog cleared from her brain. "You may proceed."

Nick shook his head. "You need help."

"No." She lifted the sad excuse for a cup. "Just a bigger mug."

Nick scraped the last bite of eggs on his plate. "Lionel's going to drive you and Rita to the hospital."

"Don't I look trustworthy?"

"I don't want Rita left alone for a second. Lionel will worry about the driving and parking. That'll leave you free to take care of Rita."

"You're not coming with us?" He was so hands-on when it came to Rita, that missing this appointment surprised her. At least he trusted her to take care of Rita at the hospital.

Frowning as if he had a headache of his own, Nick glanced at his watch and rose. "I have a meeting I can't put off."

"I'll call you the second I know anything," she offered.

He looked at her strangely, as if he hadn't expected her to realize he'd want to know right away. "Thank you. You have an interview with Alma Nisbitt this afternoon?"

"At one." How had he found out?

"I'll meet you back here at noon then."

"No need to rush back on my account."

"I want to be there."

She sighed. She had promised to help him find answers. If she wanted him to trust her, she had to give a little. "Fine."

After Nick left, Holly brought a plate of steaming

scrambled eggs and placed it in front of Valerie without a word, leaving just as silently as she'd come in.

"Spooky how she does that, don't you think?" Mike asked.

"This whole house has something off about it. Did you hear about the ghost last night?"

"Yeah, that Evan dude wasn't too happy about it. Thinks it's a joke on him."

"No, I think it was meant as a distraction."

Mike's gaze jerked up, interested. "Oh, yeah? From what?"

"I'm not sure." Just for the memory card? That seemed a little elaborate and rather hit-and-miss. How could anyone know she and Nick would be there or what they'd talk about?

"So you're going to let Tsar Nicolas tag along again?"

She shrugged, picking at the eggs. Her taste buds had gone haywire since she'd arrived here. Even with the gooey Cheddar, the eggs had a metallic taste to them. "He's not that bad."

"Worse, from what I hear."

"Who's your source?"

Mike screwed up his face and waved a hand about. "You know how it is, people talk."

"Either way, we have a job to do. The interview with Alma Nisbitt is set for one. I still haven't reached Brent Weir, but his landlady says he usually gets home from his shift at the kennel around five. Make sure all of your batteries are charged and that you have plenty of tape for both."

Mike shoved his empty plate away. "This is such a waste of my time."

"A couple more days."

Mike grumbled. "Zoe isn't going to wait around for me forever."

"She will if she's right for you."

Valerie gave up on the eggs and poured a refill of coffee instead. Her stomach was still tender and not up to solid food right now. "I should go see if Rita's ready to go."

THE MOONHILL COUNTRY CLUB was located on the western edge of town. The fieldstone-and-weathered-clapboard building had incorporated a century-old barn and its red roof into the design. The former barn now housed electric golf carts and a top-of-the-line pro shop. When Nick arrived at the restaurant, whose floor-to-ceiling windows offered a breathtaking view of Mount Monadnock, Emma Hanley was already seated and enjoying a cup of coffee.

Cripes, this was the last place he wanted to be. This scam was the last thing he wanted to discuss. Especially if his suspicions were on target.

"Nicolas! I'm so pleased to see you. How is Rita doing?"

Nick gave Emma a quick peck on the cheek. She smelled of lilacs and hair spray. "Rita looked better this morning. Dr. Marzan has her at the hospital so he can run a battery of tests."

Switch red hair for the blond and Emma was a carbon copy of Rita. No surprise there. The women had grown up together, had the same friends, went to the same schools and married within the same elite circle. Both were widowed. And both genuinely cared for people and invested a lot of their free time and money to bettering the lives of others. Between them they'd put on enough fundraisers to build and maintain the local family shelter that served a large number of women and children in need.

Rita and Emma were much too nice for him to allow them to fall for a scam. And this Valentine Pond project was a pyramid about to topple.

Nick deposited his briefcase next to the table and took the seat across from Emma. Emma signaled a waiter who hurried to fill Nick's coffee cup. The delicate china made him think of Valerie and her pained look at the tiny cups Rita preferred, and a hint of a smile tugged at his lips.

"The timing couldn't be worse," Emma said, referring to Rita's illness. "With Valentina's anniversary coming up…"

"Too much stress," Nick agreed. "I'd like to show you something before Mr. Stokke arrives."

"Oh?"

"Rita asked me to run the numbers on the Valentine Pond project." He bent down to retrieve a file from his briefcase. That's what he liked about numbers. Nothing emotional about them. Sure someone could try to fudge them, but the truth was still there for anyone willing to dig. Firmly pushing away where these numbers could lead, Nick plowed on. "Stokke Development, Inc. is nothing more than a roach motel."

Emma arched her perfectly painted eyebrows. "What do you mean?"

"Money goes in, but nothing comes out."

"But Phase One of the project went so well. I doubled my money in little more than three months. Didn't you see the homes going up on your drive in?"

"I saw one finished house and a bunch of cleared lots. That's what he wants you to see. An illusion. You were one of the first investors in, so you got your money back. What he was counting on was your good word of mouth to round up more investors." Nick pointed at the graph that all but shouted flameout. "Look here. No growth. No liquidity. He's burning through the cash he's rounded up, but there's nothing to show for it. Didn't you wonder about the lack of construction? Even the finished house is nothing more than a shell. Nothing's been done on the inside."

"Well, yes, but Mr. Stokke had a perfectly good explanation."

"What did he say?"

"Something about higher yields." She smiled sheepishly. "He was very convincing. And his numbers and charts painted a much different picture than yours."

Of course he'd know just the right angle to take with his marks. He knew his territory, knew how to pitch and knew how to close the deal. Too bad none of the marks could see past the charm and into the cold eyes. There was no conscience there, no sense of responsibility for all the chaos he'd cause. To him, they were all suckers who deserved what they got for their greed.

"When the scheme gets to the topple point," Nick said, biting back the anger that Emma didn't deserve, "you'll find that Mr. Stokke and the money will both disappear. The sale of that one house and the land won't come close to paying back everyone who's put up money. I really think you should get out of this before the whole thing falls apart. I've advised Rita against investing."

"The real estate market is so high right now." Emma's forehead crimped with deep furrows. "My advisor told me it was a good investment."

"The bubble's already bursting. And Stokke isn't playing by the rules."

Emma squinted at the numbers. "I can't believe I was taken in like that."

"Like you said, he was very convincing, and he knows how to manipulate the numbers to make his pitch sound great. But I dug beneath the surface. There's nothing there but sleight of hand." Nick leaned forward, his mouth suddenly dry. "Can I ask you what this Carter Stokke looks like?"

"He's a charming man. He has an explosive smile, bright and bulging with confidence. When he smiles, his green irises lighten to jade and sparkle." She blushed like a schoolgirl. "Listen to me. You'd think I was smitten."

Nick pulled an old photograph from his briefcase and refused to look at it as he passed it to Emma. He never thought about that person anymore. "Is this the man?"

Emma coyly put on reading glasses and examined the picture. "Why, yes. I mean, he looks younger in this picture. His hair is a handsome silver now and his face more mature. But, yes, I'd say that's the same man. Do you know him?"

"Unfortunately, yes." The sour bile that had kept Nick

small and sickly as a child returned with a vengeance and curdled the contents of his stomach. "He's my father. And he's nothing more than a crook."

Chapter Ten

The air inside Alma Nisbitt's doll-size house in downtown Moonhill was thick and sullen and reminded Valerie of a funeral parlor before the grievers arrived. Which didn't help her stomach any. A low-level nausea had roiled around her gut all morning while she'd waited for Rita at the hospital and showed no signs of leaving. She chewed on another Pepto-Bismol tablet and concentrated on Alma.

Tiny squares and triangles of fabric in a wash of stained glass colors littered a small table near the window. A stack of baby quilts in various stages of finishing were piled in a chair in the corner. Alma had worked busily at the sewing table when Valerie, Nick and Mike had arrived, her sewing machine chugging like an electric train as if the faster she sewed, the faster she could put back together the lost pieces of her life.

Alma now sat in a maple rocking chair in her living room, a cup of instant coffee balanced on her knees, her apple face pruned unkindly by time. Her small fingers jittered against the turquoise melamine of her cup and her gaze kept snapping back to her sewing table as if she were on some sort of deadline she hated to miss.

Mike set up his camera and clipped a mic to the yellowed Peter Pan collar of Alma's dress.

Nick stood just inside Valerie's peripheral vision, keeping up the wall to Alma's kitchen entrance with his shoulder, arms crossed over his chest, tension lapping off him in ripples.

Something had gone wrong with his morning meeting. Not that he was going to share his concerns. She had no reason to let it bother her, either, except that she'd become attuned to his moods in a way she never had with anyone else. *Get over yourself, Valerie.* He had his business to run. It had nothing to do with her. And she had a package to put together and three days left to do the job. She couldn't let his dark vibes drive her crazy. He was never going to trust her. He was never going to trust anybody.

Valerie sat in a straight chair in front of Alma and started with a few questions designed to put her at ease, but Alma would have none of it.

"Cut the small talk," Alma interrupted, lips pinched. "You want to know about Stanley."

Though the subject was obviously painful to Alma, Valerie admired her directness. "Yes, I would."

"Stanley was a good man." Alma's gaze went right through Valerie to some unknown place only Alma could see. "He served Rita well. She had no complaints."

"I've heard he was a loyal employee," Valerie said, seeking to show Alma she was not the enemy.

"He loved her. We all did." Alma dug a lacy handkerchief

from the pocket of her dress and proceeded to worry its edge.

Valerie nudged her. "He was Rita's landscaper."

Alma's face lit up. "Oh, he brought those gardens into glorious beauty!"

"I've seen pictures. The grounds were exquisitely kept."

Alma's gaze narrowed. "But you're not here to talk about the magic Stanley made with his plants and flowers. You're here about that night."

Valerie nodded. "The night Valentina disappeared."

"He didn't do what he said he did. He didn't kidnap that child. He knew what it was like to have your child taken away." Tears glossed Alma's faded blue eyes. "We suffered through three stillbirths before the doctor said we shouldn't try anymore. Three times we buried our babies. Three times we had our hearts broken."

"I'm so sorry to hear that."

The lace of Alma's handkerchief frayed under her busy fingers. "My Stanley, he was a good man, and he loved Rita. He hated to see her suffer the way she was. Ten years ago, he was dying. Cancer. Melanoma. From all his days out in the sun. But Stanley wasn't one to listen to anybody. He did things his way. He figured if he confessed to kidnapping Valentina, and if he said she died before he could give her back, then Rita could go on with her life. I could've told him it wouldn't be enough."

"The body?" Valerie asked. "Where did Stanley say he buried it?"

A slow run of tears slid down Alma's cheeks. "I've watched those crime shows. I know that there's not much hope of finding kids alive if they've been missing for more than a couple of days. It'd been years. She had to be dead. But they never found a body. Stanley said he sent it down the river on a raft, but he just wanted to help Rita. She was always so good to him. To us. Even after the drinking got bad."

"Stanley had a drinking problem," Valerie said, keeping all accusation out of her voice. The police investigation into Stanley's confession had proven Alma's claim of Stanley's innocence to be true. But that wouldn't have stopped Nick. How many times had he had the river dragged for evidence of that raft, of a body—just in case?

Alma took in a deep breath. "He wanted a son of his own so badly. After our third baby—a boy—when the doctor said we shouldn't try again or I could die, Stanley went a little crazy."

Crazy enough to kidnap Valentina? He couldn't possibly think he could just give her to his wife and get away with it? Had he wanted the ransom to buy a baby of his own? Had something happened to Valentina before he could return her unharmed? "A little crazy how?"

"He was drunk that night. Like he'd been for almost a month. I got mad at him for drowning his sorrows. I had sorrows, too, you know. He wasn't the only one who was crushed by the news. Here's the man I loved more than anything in the world, and I couldn't give him the one thing he wanted." Alma slapped the torn handkerchief at her tears. "Anyway, I needed someone to feel sorry for me, so I went to my sister's in Concord and left him to get himself plastered. I knew I'd be fine in a couple of days. I'd come back. We'd patch things up."

"So you weren't home the night Valentina was kidnapped?" Valerie asked.

Alma gulped. "No, but Stanley told me about it. About how he'd seen someone creeping into the woods with a sack on his back. He tried to run after him, but he tripped and knocked himself out coming out of the gardening shed."

Behind Valerie, Nick's breathing sped up. Was Alma's tale reviving his memory? "Did Stanley say anything else about the man?"

Alma shook her head. "No, just that he was big and dressed all in black. My Stanley, he never drank a single drop after that night. He paid for his mistake. He was a good man."

"He tried to help Valentina," Valerie agreed, as much for Nick as for Alma.

Alma nodded. "He said he was lying there on the ground and he could hear her bawling, but he couldn't get up. Valentina's cries haunted him until the day he died."

"Valentina was crying?" Nick asked. The shards of tension splintering from him prickled through Valerie's body like sharpened needles.

Alma twirled the cup in its saucer. "He said he thought she was calling out for help."

Valerie turned in her chair and a cold, tight ball formed inside her chest at the sight of Nick. His stricken gaze met hers in an instant and familiar connection, and the movie from the tower room rolled by much too vividly in her mind, including the end she hadn't seen before because he'd scared her so badly. Why did Valentina insist on haunting her this way?

The little boy's eyes black with panic. His mouth open wide, a scream frozen in his throat. His limbs shaking under the blanket, his arms reaching out helplessly to Valentina.

If Valentina was crying outside in the night, then that meant she was alive after she left the house, not dead as Nick had believed for all those years.

He would pack on another layer of blame he didn't deserve. She wanted to go to him, to hold him, to tell him he couldn't have altered the course of events that night. Maybe that's what Valentina wanted her to do—let Nick know he wasn't responsible. But he wouldn't thank her for making his weakness public, and she had a job to finish. They would talk later.

Sending him one last understanding glance, she turned back to Alma.

If Valentina had been alive, that changed everything.

As NICK DROVE AWAY from Alma Nisbitt's house, frustration hummed across his skin like the electric current therapy he'd had for tendonitis in his shoulder a few years back.

None of the reports he'd paid a small fortune for had spelled out that Stanley Nisbitt had heard Valentina cry out for help. But Valerie's questions had freed the secret Alma had kept for her husband all these years.

Add that revelation to the one he'd made this morning, and Nick didn't like the picture the pieces were forming.

Gordon Archer, aka Carter Stokke this time around, was back and his real estate scheme was a smoke screen. He was after revenge—just as he'd promised Holly twenty-six years ago when Nick's mother had left him. He'd vowed to destroy her and everyone who'd helped her, including Rita.

Was he the one who'd taken Valentina? What better way to ruin Rita's life? A child for a child. That would make twisted sense to someone like Gordon.

In Gordon's skewed sense of values, people willingly gifted him what he'd "earned." But that was many years and many prison terms ago. Would he resort to violence now?

Valentina was alive after she'd left the tower room. Had Gordon sold her to hurt Rita? What was his plan now? Did he want something more than to separate Rita from her cash in a bad investment?

If Valentina was alive, then Nick had tried to bury the wrong ghost for all these years.

He peeled onto Main Street past Memorial Square. "Where to?"

"I need coffee," Valerie moaned. One hand clamped on her stomach, she wound down the window and breathed in the cool afternoon air.

She didn't look well. "You've had too much coffee already. No wonder your stomach hurts." He handed her the bottle of water he always kept handy. "Here. You need hydration."

He ground his teeth and focused on the road.

Valentina's bloody face kept reappearing against the black canvas.

He could have saved her. She'd been alive.

Cripes, she'd cried for help, and he'd been stone and ice watching her disappear.

"I could use a bite to eat," Mike grumbled from the back.

Nick shook his head, tearing apart the dark mirror of memory. "I don't know how you people get any work done."

The memory seeped in again. Everything he'd believed in all these years was suddenly turned around. All that blood. Those dead eyes. The limp body.

She'd cried. He hadn't heard her. She'd been afraid. He'd done nothing to help her. She'd called out to him, and he'd lain frozen in place under her pink blanket in the tower room. The thought of her horror as she'd been dragged farther and farther from her home squirmed like bait through his gut.

He could've saved her. If he'd only—

Valerie squeezed his knee. "You're going to drive yourself crazy with all the 'what-ifs.'"

The golden dusk gathering at the window swam in her hair and he wanted to plunge his hands into that inviting silk, forget all the horrors darkening his mind. Back at Alma's house, she'd seemed to understand him on a gut level, and she was doing it again, reading him like a profit-and-loss statement. This growing connection between them was a problem. Separating his feelings from his duty was becoming harder. She looked too much like Valentina would. She was the wrong person to turn to.

Was that why Valerie was here? Was Valentina's ghost speaking through her to lead him to the truth?

He'd been around the professor too much to come around to *that* conclusion. Not that much made any sense at this point.

There was nothing he could do with the information Alma Nisbitt had given him until he got in touch with Joe later tonight and gave him this new direction for a search.

Nick goosed the gas pedal and the engine growled into life along the deserted stretch of 202. "What's the address we're looking for?"

With a crook of her eyebrow Valerie gave him Brent Weir's address. Nick steered the car toward Peterborough, concentrating on the road, on the changing colors of the leaves, on the gushing waters along the Contoocook River—on anything but the sympathy on Valerie's face.

"Brent Weir was nineteen when Rita hired him to replace a retiring chauffeur." Valerie scraped a thumbnail along the edge of the closed file folder on her lap.

She glanced at him sideways as if measuring his mental health. What did she think he was going to do? Commit hara-kiri to atone for his sins? A quick and easy death wasn't an option for him. Never had been. He'd given his all to protect Rita and his mother and had hoped that, one day, he'd bring Valentina's body home where she belonged and give them both a form of closure. He'd assumed he'd seen her die. All the information he'd gathered had agreed with that conclusion.

But what if she'd lived?

"Brent had been on the job for only six months and

pulled a disappearing act the night Valentina was kidnapped," Valerie continued. "That put him at the top of the
suspect list for a while."

A vague image of the chauffeur formed on the edge of
Nick's memory. As polished as the Bentley he drove for
Rita, young Brent had looked sharp in his crisp uniform
and shiny car. He could talk about engines and horse-
power and performance with Nick's father. But he'd also
hated Valentina's constant reel of questions, and so Nick
had hated him in return—especially after Brent had turned
the hose on Valentina one spring day, then laughed as if it
was all a big joke.   ·

"Come on, kid. Can't you take a joke?"

A sopping wet and hiccuping Valentina stood in
the middle of the garage crescent where Brent was
washing the cars until Nick tugged on her hand.
"Hey, wanna see something cool?"

She sniffed. "What?"

"It's a secret." He bent close to her ear so Brent
wouldn't hear. "You have to promise to be quiet or
you'll scare them away."

That pricked her attention. Her body softened
and her hand slid companionably into his. "What is
it, Nick? What is it?"

"You'll see."

He led her toward the pond and the little cove
he'd discovered last week. As he got close to the
special spot, he put a finger against his lips. "Shh."

He got down on his belly on the tall grass and

urged Valentina to do the same. She giggled as they crabbed toward the reeds and the duck's nest he'd meant to keep to himself. Five fat eggs rested under the Mama duck and, as they watched, one of the shells started to crack.

"Oh, Nick, look!" And with wonder in her big, blue eyes, she'd watched the duckling peck its way into the world and forgotten all about Brent and his cruel joke.

"The police found out Brent had learned that day that his fifteen-year-old girlfriend was pregnant," Valerie said. "The girl's father threatened to have Brent arrested for statutory rape if he didn't marry her."

"Sounds like a real peach," Mike said. "He's not going to want to talk?"

"He ended up marrying the girl and they divorced a year later." Valerie turned in her seat to look at Mike. "You never know. He might."

"I'll bet you ten bucks that bringing up a marriage that started with the business end of a shotgun is going to get you a door slammed in your face."

"We have to try."

Brent lived on the bottom floor of a pale blue triple-decker that had rental stamped all over it. The bare necessities were there, but no extras that made a house a home. Yellowed grass in need of a cut ran from curb to foundation. They walked up a cracked concrete walkway to a plain white front door, grayed by dirt from the street.

The forty-three-year-old version of Brent Weir was like

a poster used by high school health teachers to warn students against drug use. Whatever good looks he'd had twenty-five years ago were long gone. A soft belly hung over his belt. Cuts and bruises marked the backs of his hands. He hadn't changed from his day job and his stained jeans and sweatshirt smelled like a dirty kennel and sour resentment.

He spotted Mike's camera as soon as he opened the door and his expression darkened. "What do you want?"

"I'm Valerie Zea from WMOD-TV in Orlando. I'd like to talk to you about the night of Valentina—" Valerie started.

Brent's meaty hand turned white against the door frame and his face quaked with rage. "Leave me alone, bitch. I don't need no finger pointed at me for something I didn't even do. I didn't kidnap neither of them kids."

"There was more than one?" Valerie asked.

Brent spit a wad of tobacco juice at her feet. "As if you didn't know. She sent you, didn't she?"

"Who?"

"That bitch Hillary, that's who." Brent leaned forward into Valerie's face. Nick stepped up to stand next to Valerie. If Brent so much as breathed too hard on her, he'd end up on his can. "Hil thinks she can use the anniversary to make me crack. It ain't gonna work. You can go to hell. All of you."

Brent slammed the door in their faces. The impact shook the entire house and loosened the iron six tacked to the door, turning it into a low-hanging nine.

"Did you know about the other missing child?" Valerie asked Nick as they got back in the car. In the early evening's light, the row of houses cast shadows like crooked fangs along the street. "That wasn't in Rita's files."

"If I remember, Weir was cleared." Nick snapped on the headlights. He'd read about the second disappearance, but couldn't remember the details. "I'll have my investigator look into it."

"You have an investigator?" She snorted. "Of course you do."

"Do you know how many people have claimed to be the missing Valentina?" As the car rolled down the narrow street, the streetlights strobed over Valerie's face in a Mardi Gras mask effect: black, white, black, white. The car's interior was suddenly too small as a parade of ghosts joined Valerie in her seat. Pretenders. Each one promising Rita deliverance only to implant another thorn of guilt in Nick's heart. He couldn't breathe through the wound of reliving his nightmare so many times.

"How many?" Valerie asked softly.

"Thirteen." He slanted her an accusing glance. He was tired of fighting, he realized, tired of destroying Valentina over and over again. He just wanted her to lie in peace. "Fourteen, if I count you."

"I never claimed to be Valentina."

"Which makes yours the most cruel con of all."

Hurt flickered in Valerie's eyes and stabbed him in the chest.

"Hey! Valerie's the most honest person I know." Mike's hands clasped both headrests and he pulled himself forward. "She could have gone further in her career if she'd been willing to fudge a little. But it's always the truth with her."

"Not helping, Mike." Valerie frowned at Mike, then turned back to Nick. "You had me investigated. You know I'm telling the truth."

"He had you investigated?" Mike whipped his head from Valerie to Nick. "What about me?"

"You, too," Nick said. "Just like anyone who stays at Moongate."

Mike's gaze narrowed. "Find anything interesting?"

A muscle in Nick's jaw twitched as he clenched his teeth. "You need to learn to save more. Retirement is going to sneak up on you faster than you think."

"Thanks for the tip." Mike huffed and shoved back into his seat. "Here's one for you. You can't mess with people the way you do. You can't look at Valerie one minute like you're going to eat her up, then scowl at her the next like you're going to bite her head off. You hurt her and you're going to have to answer to me."

"I'll keep that in mind." Nick stopped at the traffic light. The stop signal bathed the inside of the car red, and he imagined that this red haze was what a bull saw before he charged.

Mike had it wrong. Nick didn't want to eat Valerie up. He didn't want to bite her head off. He simply wanted her gone.

But he couldn't trust his memory. He couldn't trust his instincts. He couldn't trust anything right now, least of all himself.

He didn't want to trust Valerie. But he had no choice. With her prying questions and her Valentina look, she was the one person, he was beginning to realize, who could make him see the face of the monster of his nightmares and lead him to the truth.

Chapter Eleven

Nick wrenched himself awake, ripping into consciousness just to escape the nightmare. It scraped and scratched at the back of his brain, ready to pounce on him again. All he had to do was close his eyes and he'd pitch right back into its waiting hell. With the heels of his hands against his eyes, he tried to scrub away the painful memories.

He'd spent his day at the carriage house—away from Valerie, her constant questions and her nasty coffee addiction. He'd alternated his time between tracking down investors of the Valentine Pond project from a list Emma Hanley had given him to warn them about Stokke's scheme, and running down information about the second child who'd gone missing six months after Valentina.

Someone had snatched Hillary Clark's infant daughter from her crib on her second night home from the hospital. Just like Valentina, the baby seemed to have vanished off the face of the earth. No trace of her was ever found—not alive, not dead.

As the baby's father, Brent Weir was questioned, but he'd provided a solid alibi and was released. The media had done their best to stir fear in parents' hearts with head-lines pronouncing that a serial child snatcher roamed the area. But with Kirby Cicco already in custody for Valentina's kidnapping, the police had no proof that the two crimes were related.

Nick hadn't meant to fall asleep. He'd meant to rest his eyes for a few minutes before going back to work—to shed the crushing weight of all his past ghosts coming back to haunt him. Just a few minutes before dinner to clear his head. Instead, he'd fallen into the dream's well-worn tracks of darkness and death, of ice and blood.

Panting, he sat on the edge of the bed, hands hanging down between his knees.

Under the constant cuff of wind the entire carriage house creaked, and the windows seemed to exhale, blowing cold into the room.

A storm was coming, and he couldn't stop it.

How many times had he almost gone to Valerie today? How many times had he wanted to compare notes or get her take on something? Dependency—another sign of weakness.

He couldn't afford to be weak now.

Not with Gordon Archer—Nick couldn't think of the man as his father—back in town. He had no conscience and didn't give using people's hopes, fears and desires against them a second thought. If the suckers fell for his smooth-talking ways, then they deserved what they got. A successful con came down to knowing personal details, and Gordon was an expert at reading his marks. Valerie and her hold on Nick would give Gordon too much leverage.

He should make her leave, put her out of harm's way.
But he needed her to travel the messy maze Valentina had
left behind, and Valerie had gotten him closer to the center
than anyone else had.

Swallowing a curse, Nick jumped up. Still clad in his
shirt and pants, he padded to his office. A couple hours of
staring at financial statements would get him back on
track. It always did. In this arena no one could hide from
him, no secret could stay buried for long. In the world of
numbers, he always successfully hunted down the truth.

Soon, the anniversary would be over. Gordon's scheme
would be exposed. Valerie, her cameraman and the professor would go. And things would go back to normal.

He'd protected Rita and his mother for all these years.
He could keep Valerie safe for a few more days.

He fired up the computer, checked his mail, then got
down to work. Just as his tight neck muscles were starting
to relax, the lights flickered and died.

The darkness in him rose again, murky and deep. He
could not give in to it. Not yet.

VALERIE HAD SPENT Saturday with a telephone clamped
to her ear. Each thread she'd followed had led to a knot
that refused to unravel. How did that bode for her future
as a news producer for a New York network station or
CNN or MSNBC?

After losing the signal yet again, she launched her cell
phone at the foot of the bed and threw herself backward
onto the pillows of her bed at Moongate. With a hand, she
soothed the cramp knotting her stomach.

Why was the truth so hard to find? Not that she had much objectivity left when it came to this story. If she kept this up, the last seven years of hard work—her career— would go right onto the cutting room floor.

If she could just hang on for one more day, the story would come together. She could feel it in her bones.

She got up and stretched. What she needed was a good run to give her mind a chance to sort through all the information she'd gathered that day—not that her cranky digestion was a willing cooperator. She couldn't think of a thing she'd eaten that would warrant another sour episode like this. As bad as Holly's cooking was, it couldn't be the food, since Mike, Evan and Nick weren't complaining of bellyaches. Which left stress as the culprit.

Arms still bent overhead, she stopped midstretch. Someone was watching. The thought came to her out of nowhere. Darkness had crept up on her as she'd worked and moonlight spotlighted her in the window. "When did you turn into such a chicken?"

Laughing uneasily, she went to the window, scoured the lawn and tried to see deep into the woods. Nothing but the wind stirring tree shadows into a giant breathing spiderweb. She twitched the lace curtains shut and wished for a heavy blind.

The silence between her and Nick didn't help her tension. They were on the same side. They were looking for the same answers. Why had he refused to pool their resources and work together? He couldn't seriously still believe she was trying to scam Rita.

Speaking of difficult people. Valerie glanced at her

watch. Just past six. She couldn't put off her call to Higgins any longer. With a groan she rifled through her purse for antacid. Chewing on the chalky tablets, she picked up her phone, then cursed. Getting reception in this house was on par with playing Russian roulette.

She'd been playing chase-the-signal all day, taking calls in the most unprofessional of places—the top of a boulder, standing on a bench on the deck, leaning over a balcony at the back of the house. Although, before the wind had set in, sitting in the gazebo by the pond with the sun warming her had felt as good as a spa massage. A luxury her mother disapproved of, but one Valerie had been forced to enjoy—with multiple takes—for a segment.

With a resigned sigh, she snagged her blazer and started to scan for a signal. She was halfway up the driveway to Nick's carriage house before she found enough power to connect with Higgins. There was no answer on his office line, but he answered his cell on the third ring.

"How's it going, kiddo?" Higgins asked.

Valerie hooked a protective arm over her stomach. *Stick to the facts and you'll be okay.* "I finally got Hillary Clark to agree to an interview. It's set for tomorrow morning. The medication the doctor gave Rita is working well, and she's feeling better every day. I should be able to interview her tomorrow afternoon and catch the last flight out of Manchester." Which strangely enough didn't fill her with the usual post-shoot high.

"Tick-tock," Higgins said, reminding her of her looming deadline. "I need you back tonight. I've booked you a nine o'clock flight. Didn't Mike give you the message?"

She hadn't talked to Mike since lunch. "There's not enough time to make the airport. Do you realize how far in the sticks this place is?"

Not that bad, really, but she couldn't go back. Not with two interviews left to tape and possibly turn a ho-hum segment into something special. She'd need a straight IV of caffeine to get the copy and editing done on time once she got back to the studio, but she was *not* going to admit defeat and let Higgins promote Bailey over her because she couldn't deliver. "I'll need a day and a half to post. Tops. Maybe another afternoon to mix. You'll have your package on time."

"I need copy for Dan's V-O ASAP so we can get the promos tracked."

Why was he piling the busywork on her? The promos should've been tracked already and someone at the studio could've come up with the copy for Dan's voice-over. "I'll work on it tonight. Mike should have already sent you some B-roll of the house with a time-coded EDL for the bites I want."

Mike had shot some terrific footage of the fog-shrouded house. Together they'd gone over each frame off-line and come up with an edit decision list they'd use to put together the edited master.

"Where are you?" Higgins asked. "You sound like you're in a wind tunnel."

"Couldn't get a cell signal inside, so I'm outside freezing my butt off, putting in overtime to keep my EP in the loop." Not that said executive producer cared.

"Good girl."

"I really need the interview with Rita to make the segment work," Valerie insisted and heard the hint of a whine in her tired voice. "I'll work nonstop till it's done. You know I will."

"You're too stubborn for your own good." Higgins paused as if weighing his options. "Okay, you've got one more day."

"Thanks. You won't regret it."

"I already do."

As she hit the end button, a bone-deep sense of danger set the hairs on the back of her neck stirring in alarm. She pivoted to locate the source. Even though her sight had adjusted to the dim evening light all that surrounded her was the black shadow of tree limbs shifting like frenzied ghosts at an orgy and the pulsing waves of wind moaning through the woods. Clouds scudded across the rising moon like one of those time-lapsed clips she'd used to mark the passage of time in a previous Halloween segment, adding to her nausea.

"Just the wind," she told herself. She was in the country. Tree limbs creaking were normal and shouldn't have the hairs on the back of her neck standing upright. How did she expect to handle tougher responsibilities when she let a bit of wind scare her?

With determination, she waved the phone around, trying to find reception once again. But she could not ignore the cry of alarm screeching through every cell in her body that was quickly turning her muscles to jelly.

Then through the black of night, she spotted a light. Nick's house was right ahead, closer than the mansion. His silhouette hunched over his desk cut sharply against the background of his bright office. She nearly cried with relief at the thought of reaching Nick and safety.

Nick, look up. And the childish, *Help me, Nick,* echoed somewhere in her head, making her feel like a gutless fool.

A branch cracked. She gasped and spun around.

Finger fumbling for the Speed Dial 5 slot where she'd entered Nick's number, she hurried toward the carriage house. *You don't need him. Turn around. Go back to the mansion. There's no one out in this weather, except you.*

Before she could press the button, a black shadow sprang from behind a tree and lunged at her. She veered away from it, but the sudden heave of her stomach bent her over.

A gloved hand strapped across her mouth and yanked her back against a steel-hard chest, choking her scream and halting her in her tracks. She fought against the iron grip, but her continuing bout of stomach sourness had left her as weak as a moth. The fierce arm banded across her chest trapped her and emptied her lungs. As she struggled to breathe through the glove plastered across her mouth and nose, she tasted leather, grass and earth.

An avalanche of panic swamped her and her air-deprived brain snapped with images of Valentina in the tower room, her bleeding head pounding, her terror-filled lungs frozen, her silent scream rasping her throat raw.

Nick, Nick, Nick! Help me, Nick! A gust of wind pounded over her and the lights in Nick's office went out. *No, Nick! Help me!*

She was all alone. No one knew where she was. No one would miss her for hours.

A stinking breath chugged in Valerie's ear. "Let Valentina sleep, or you'll find your mother and your dog dead when you get home. Do you understand?"

Her blood ran cold. Oh, God, no. Not her mother. Tears stinging her eyes, Valerie nodded.

Her captor shoved her away. The world blurred and spun as she slammed against the frozen ground. Pain shot through her hip and shoulder. Her cell phone went flying out of her hand. Some part of her brain remembered to roll to break the fall.

"This is your last warning," the voice growled from somewhere above her. *"Leave."*

The ground thundered as he sped away into the woods.

Lying half on the driveway, half on the lawn, Valerie gulped air into her deprived lungs. Her fingers crept forward along the frost-crusted grass to retrieve her phone. It still worked. Tears blurring her vision, finger poised over Speed Dial 5, she was about to press the button when footsteps crunched closer.

"Stay away!" she warned. "I have pepper spray." Which she'd had to leave at home because she couldn't take it on the airplane with her, but he didn't know that.

"Valerie?"

"Nick?"

Relief flooded her and she scrambled to her feet.

Nick reached down to help her up. "What are you doing out here?"

"Oh, God, I thought he'd come back."

"Who?"

Shivering with all the adrenaline pumping through her blood, she buried her face against his collar. "Someone came out of the woods." The words tumbled out in one long rush. "He jumped me, then he said he'd kill my mother if I didn't stop this story."

Nick's muscles tensed around her. "Are you all right?"

"I'm fine." Shaken, but okay.

"We need to get out of this open space." Tucking her tight into his side, Nick ushered her toward the darkened mansion. "I'll call the police."

Now that the shaking was ebbing, she loosened her hold on his shirt and fumbled for her phone. "My mother—"

"My investigator's in Florida. I'll send him over to make sure she's all right."

"Would you?" She was too thankful to wonder for long what Nick's investigator was doing in Florida.

"Of course." He reached for her again. "Joe'll make sure nothing happens to her."

Valerie wrapped her hands around her elbows, hugging herself, denying herself the comfort he offered. "You know what this means, don't you?"

"What?"

"That we're close to the truth. The warning is proof." Her stomach started to churn again. "I can't leave. I can't let him win."

He urged her forward. "I won't. Let's get inside."

With a hand on her stomach, she nodded.

"I think you should do as he says and go home," Nick said.

She swiveled to face him. "I'm not leaving, Nick. This

is my problem, too. He threatened my mother. If I leave now, then the segment won't air, and he gets what he wants. I have to finish this."

"I'm not risking your life."

"The risk isn't yours to take."

His face turned grim and his voice dangerously low. "We'll discuss this later."

"I'm not going to change my mind."

"I can throw you out."

"I'll stay at the inn."

"I can make sure they don't take you in."

"You don't control the whole state."

With a growl, Nick pressed against the wings of her shoulders to get her moving and probed the shadows with a searching gaze. "The guy who attacked you could still be out here. I'd feel better inside."

Taking in a deep breath, she shook her head. "He knows you'll call the cops. He's long gone. You go on ahead. There's no cell reception inside, and I need to hear my mother's voice."

"I'm not leaving you out here when security's compromised. You can use the inside phone. The lines are still up. I just called the electric company."

With a relief she'd never admit out loud, she hung on to Nick's hand with a bit too much force as he led her into the dark mansion to the small windowless den Holly used as an office. For all Valerie's tough talk, the attack had scared her spitless. She didn't breathe fully again until Nick had set up an oil lamp to light the room and chase away the pitch of night.

"I have to check on Rita and get the generator running." Nick's expression was too somber and tense as he studied her. "You'll be okay?"

"I'm fine." She forced a smile and tucked a windblown strand of hair behind her ear. "Thanks for everything."

At the doorway, Nick hesitated, tapped the door frame once, then left.

Valerie paced the den as far as the telephone cord would let her and called her mother. "Mom?"

"What's wrong, Valerie?"

Everything! Her career-making assignment was turning into a nightmare. How could she admit to her mother that her job—a job her mother was constantly warning her against—had put them both in danger? Reverting back to an old habit, she chewed on a thumbnail. "Nothing. I just wanted to make sure you were all right."

"As well as can be expected when I'm not living in my own space."

Too worried about her mother's safety to take offense, Valerie ignored her mother's suffering tone. "Hey, I just remembered I forgot to tell you that the lock on the back door is sticky. Make sure you double-check it before you go to bed."

"It's Saturday, Valerie. In a few hours, it'll be Sunday."

Valerie swallowed a mouthful of guilt. "I'll be home on Monday at the latest, Mom. I promise. How's Luna doing?"

"You'll have two noise-ordinance citations to pay when you get home," her mother said in a pinched tone. "But it's raining tonight."

Would the rain keep an intruder away or give him

enough cover to abet his task? Her mother was too frugal to "waste" money on a hotel. Last Valerie had heard her mother's cousin—the only other family she had—was in the middle of relocating. And if Valerie told her mother about the threat, her mother would insist on a showdown. Nobody, but nobody threatened her baby and got away with it. Never mind that the threat was against *her*. Valerie had learned to edit what she told her mother a long time ago. Which left her with only one option—protecting her without her knowledge. "It's windy here, Mom, and the power's out. I'll call you tomorrow. Be careful, okay?"

Valerie put in one more call to her friend Sheree's brother. He was a cop. She told him about the threat she'd just received and about the investigator Nick was sending. By promising Sheree's brother a date when she got back, she got him to keep a second set of eyes on her mother until Valerie returned tomorrow night.

Her mother would be all right. Within fifteen minutes she'd have a cop bodyguard. Nick would send his investigator. Luna's hair-trigger yodel would wake up the whole neighborhood.

Besides Valerie knew of no one as tough as her mother. Valerie had seen a hardened patrol cop cower in fear when he'd tried to ticket her mother for speeding after he'd tailgated her into going faster than the limit. He'd been willing to let her off on a warning. She'd insisted on a court date, and even the judge had gone out of his way to get her out of his courtroom in record time.

Nobody could sneak up on her, either. God knew Valerie had tried all the tricks over the years. And since

Valerie's father had died two years ago, her mother slept with a gun she knew how to use with deadly precision.

Her mother was safe. Running back home now would only bury the truth deeper.

VALERIE'S ATTACK pecking at his mind, Nick strode to the kitchen, which would lead him to the generator. He bowled into Gardner, coming up the basement stairs.

Gardner puffed up proud. "I have your answer."

"Great," Nick said as he tried to squeeze by.

Clueless, the professor anchored himself on the door frame. "There's no ghost. As I suspected, it's infrasound traveling up a pipe close to the sump pump. The motor runs rough, expending a huge amount of unneeded energy that's causing the infrasonic wave."

Suppressing a growl, Nick asked, "Then why does the baby cry only when the door is closed?"

"Because then the doorjamb is supported and vibrates at the right frequency to make the movement audible. Which also explains why it's localized to the tower room. In the day you don't hear it because of the ambient noises, but at night when everything's quiet, the noise travels."

Nick couldn't give a flip about ghosts or infrasound. He wanted the power back on. He wanted the perimeter shored up. More than anything, he wanted Valerie safe. "Send me your report."

Gardner sputtered, less than pleased with Nick's reaction to his revelation.

Nick pushed by the professor and descended the stairs,

the beam of his flashlight whirling a macabre dance on the walls.

Nick had lived with an abuser long enough to recognize the hidden meaning behind every word, the implied threat behind every inflection, the imminent action behind every twitch of body language. Once the hitting started, only blood would stop it.

Gardner might have solved the mystery of the ghost, but a greater danger lurked nearby, waiting for one moment of inattention on Nick's part to destroy his world.

HE COULDN'T LET the bastard take this away from him. Not after all the work he'd put into this venture. He couldn't let them win. Again. He deserved that money. He deserved his reward.

He wasn't a cruel man. He'd tried to get what was his without hurting anyone. A few hundred thousand dollars wouldn't wipe out any of those greedy investors. It was mere pocket change for them. A joke they would laugh off when they all got together for their next cocktail party.

But now all bets were off.

He would silence her—as he should have long ago. Bury his mistake.

He would take what she owed him for all the grief she'd caused him.

With one last play, he would solve all of his problems.

Chapter Twelve

By the time Valerie had finished her calls, Nick and Lionel had the generator running and the mansion lit up as if nothing was out of the ordinary.

Nick checked in with Holly, helped the nurse install Rita in the library, then dealt with the police. He left soon after, skipping dinner and saying something about checking on security. Valerie worried that he was patrolling the grounds alone, looking for her attacker.

After dinner, Rita claimed she was feeling better and insisted Valerie do her interview in the library while they had tea. She'd applied makeup artfully and dressed in a cyan-blue pantsuit that would look good on camera. Her champagne hair was combed back into an elegant chignon. Her skin still looked too pale and drawn, but an inner strength shone above the physical weakness.

"It's late," Valerie said. "Are you sure you're up to an interview tonight?"

"I've slept all day." Rita poured herself a cup of tea. "I won't be able to sleep again for hours."

"Nick won't like that he's not here." Valerie shuffled the notes she already knew by heart. "I should call him."

Rita tasted her tea, then added sugar. "Please don't. I'd prefer he not be here. Nicolas can be too protective at times."

Like Valerie's own mother. "He means well."

"I know he does." A touch of sadness clouded Rita's eyes. "I don't know how I would have survived all those years without him. He's been a blessing."

Rita had arranged for this segment and her uncle had granted her the resources she'd wanted. Valerie had to respect Rita's wishes to put Valentina's story out there. Without Nick hovering nearby, maybe Rita could be more open, too.

If Valerie could get this interview taped tonight, she could catch an earlier flight and relieve some of the pressure of getting this package to Higgins on time. And the faster she got this story on air, the faster her attacker's threats against her mother would stop. And, she hoped, the faster he would become a guest of the department of corrections and give Rita the resolution she'd sought.

"Nick's been living at Moongate for a long time," Valerie said while Mike set up his camera.

He was so quiet that Valerie doubted Rita was aware of his presence. He had the uncanny knack of being able to fade into the background when he was shooting. Valerie had gotten some incredible shots because of that ability.

"Nicolas has been living here since he was five," Rita said. "He and Holly came to stay here at the mansion— about a year before…Valentina disappeared."

"What happened to Nick's father?" Valerie was digressing from her goal, but she couldn't seem to help herself.

"He went to prison. Fraud. The wretched man was charming but selfish. Holly worked her fingers to the bone trying to make a home for him. And what did he do? He gambled their future away every night. That he had a wife and child to support seemed to make no difference to him."

No wonder Nick was so touchy about being taken in by a scam artist.

Mike gave her the at-speed signal. Valerie started out with nonquestions to ease Rita into the conversation.

"Your daughter was born in October, yet you named her Valentina."

The smile wiped ten years off Rita's face, shed it of its brittle mask of sadness. "It was my mother's name. She'd died the year before, and I missed her horribly. Valentina Stefania Meadows Callahan. That's such a mouthful for a baby! So I called her Tina when it was just the two of us."

"Tina, come with me. I have something to show you." Mama's eyes twinkled like stars at night.

"What, Mama?" Bubbles fizzed in Valentina's belly like soda in a glass. Mama made the best surprises.

"Your very own big girl room." The door to the tower room whooshed open.

"Oh!" Valentina slapped both hands to her mouth.

"Do you like it?"

Valentina nodded and her breath gushed out. "It's a fairy princess room!"

A race of shivers swept over Valerie's arms. She was letting Valentina's lingering spirit get to her again. "Tell me about Valentina's father."

"Rushton Callahan. He was quite a catch in his day. Oh, your father was a handsome man. Tall, too." Rita leaned her head and seemed to measure Valerie. "You should have grown taller. The reconstructionist told me you'd be at least five-six."

Valerie shot back in her chair. Nick would have her head. If Rita still thought she was Valentina, then Rita wasn't well enough yet to do an interview. "Both my parents are on the short side."

Rita didn't seem to hear her. "I've noticed that you have your father's good heart, but also his tendency toward caution. He never liked to take risks and that kept him from achieving as much as he could have. If you're going to succeed in your chosen field, Tina, you're going to have to act with more courage. You're going to have to trust that you can succeed."

Valerie glanced at Mike, who simply shrugged, leaving the decision up to her. Rita was wrong, she wasn't a pushover. When it came to work, she could be as cutthroat as anyone else. And although she'd agreed to pretend she was Valentina when Rita was so sick a few days ago, she didn't like continuing the charade now. It seemed a cruel thing to do to a woman who'd already had her hope slashed so many times. "Maybe we should do this tomorrow."

Rita slid her teacup onto the coffee table. "I'm sorry, dear. I've frightened you."

Frightened wasn't the half of it. Valerie was falling into

the same twisting vortex she'd plunged into in the tower room the night Nick had kissed her. Emotions that couldn't be hers tossed her deeper into the spinning tornado and, when it spit her out, she was going to crash hard.

"I didn't mean to scare you," Rita said tenderly. "I know it'll take time for you to get used to the truth. Let's continue. I think we should talk about that night."

Unable to speak, Valerie nodded.

"I'll start with the party…."

Rita went on to describe the preparations, the games of pin-the-tail-on-the-donkey and musical chairs, the blue butterfly-shaped cake, the fun all the children and parents were having. Her descriptions were so vivid that Valerie could hear the bright music, taste the sweet icing and feel the happy laughter rippling all around her.

Valerie shook her head, dissolving the gauzy montage of images. Why were they so vivid? Maybe the stress of this story and Valentina's spirit were starting to affect her mind. Maybe Higgins was right and Bailey did deserve the promotion. Forcing herself to concentrate, she edged the conversation toward the moment Rita had realized that Valentina was gone.

The memory wrenched Rita's face and tears flowed freely as she described the chaos of the search, the police investigation and the ransom demand's arrival. "Rushton put the ransom together and followed the directions given by the kidnapper to the letter. But right before he reached the exchange destination, he was stopped by an officer for speeding."

Rita uttered a small cry. "Speeding! How could he go

a mile above the speed limit when Valentina's life was on the line?" Her voice cracked in two. "The officer's presence frightened the kidnapper, and Rushton wasn't able to save our daughter."

Valerie rubbed the knot tightening her chest at the thought of Rushton's anguish as he raced desperately to save his little girl. "The kidnapper never made another ransom demand?"

She shook her head. "But I have it ready to go. I never gave up hope. And I was right. Here you are, back after all those years."

Poor Rita. All this reminiscence had locked her back into the past. Valerie pulled out a few tissues from her purse and handed them to her. "You look tired. We should stop."

Rita dabbed at her tears, but continued on. "I blamed Rushton, but he blamed himself more than I ever could. He couldn't live with the constant barrage of guilt, so he left, and frankly, I was glad to have him out of the house. I was already too raw. His vast grief only served to mire mine deeper. Someone had to look for Valentina. If he wasn't up to it, then I had to take charge. She was my baby."

"Daddy! Daddy! Come play with me." Valentina rushed to her father as he walked through the front door, briefcase in hand.

He caught her flying leap into his arms. "Give me five minutes, sweet pea, then I'll take you to the park."

"Swing me high?"

Holding her by the armpits, he swung her around the foyer. The walls blurred and his big smile curved crisp dimples into his cheeks. "To the sky!"

Blinking to dissolve the clip that was tender like a bruise, Valerie asked, "What happened to him?"

A hopeless sigh reverberated through Rita's mic. "He went out for a drive one day and sped right into the Connecticut River. You could say he literally drowned in his guilt."

"Daddy, no! Daddy, come back!"

A choking sob reverberated through Valerie's whole body. She clamped her hands around her notes to stop the shaking. "How awful for both of you."

Rita flattened the damp tissues against her knee. "I'd rushed into marriage at a young age to appease my father. I didn't want to go to college. School was boring. I liked the parties and the clubs, but the rest…" She gave a short, sharp laugh. "Too bad you can't get a degree in Social Butterfly, I'd have been a shoo-in."

"So you left school and married." Valerie scoured her notes, desperate to find the thread of questions she'd lost.

A small smile full of pride tipped Rita's lips. "I gave the best parties and was a great corporate wife. I had no interest in the family business. Rushton did, and he was good to me."

Valerie sensed that this was a woman who'd laughed a lot before Valentina was kidnapped. That the whole house had once pulsed with life. Lucky Valentina.

Rita folded the damp tissues into a palm-size square

and placed it on the coffee table. "Nicolas thinks I'm gullible and easily manipulated because of my obsession with you. But a mother knows." Her gaze burned into Valerie with fervor and her hands reached for Valerie's. "And I could always feel you in my heart."

"Rita…I'm not Valentina." The last thing Valerie wanted to do was string Rita along and make her think her daughter had come back home.

"Tell me about the people who raised you." Rita's eyes were much too brilliant. Had the fever returned? "Were they good to you?"

"Rita…" Valerie shook her head helplessly. "If you think I'm Valentina, then why are you doing this interview?"

Rita's too-warm hand squeezed Valerie's as if the answer was obvious. "I'd hoped hearing all the details of your life here at Moongate would bring memories back to you. You were loved, Tina, and the heart doesn't forget love."

"What's going on here?"

Nick.

Valerie's heart thundered as she whipped around to face him.

A towering quiet palled the room. His stare could have frozen boiling water.

"This stops now," he said. "I want you and your photographer gone first thing in the morning."

THE WAY RITA HAD LOOKED at Valerie had spooked Nick. When had things gone so wrong? When had he lost control of the situation? The cold bite of wind cooled his flaming temper and by the time he reached the haven of his house, the urge to hit something had mostly passed.

A man wasn't supposed to admit to fear, but fear was the only thing that could explain the quicksand way he'd lost control in front of Rita and Valerie. Only fear could explain why he'd roared like a crazed lion, every primal instinct roused to fight.

Why he'd acted like his father.

In that moment when he'd seen Rita reach out to Valerie, he'd realized two things: he'd made a terrible mistake in asking Valerie to play Valentina to give Rita a reason to live, and his mistake had handed his father the tool for his revenge. In that instant, he'd seen the world he'd worked so hard to build and protect crack right before his eyes.

The tremor of a renewed need to roar growled in his chest.

If Gordon saw the attachment, if he knew how much Valerie had come to mean to Rita, then he wouldn't hesitate to use Valerie to hurt Rita. Especially now that Nick had ground Gordon's scheme to a halt, foiling Gordon's attempt to lighten Rita's holdings. Had he really thought Nick would allow him to get to Rita so easily? But then Gordon had always had more confidence than game.

Valerie was safe inside the mansion. Lionel, Holly and Mike were there. The generator would keep the extra security measures he'd had installed working and give him plenty of notice should anyone try to trespass onto the estate. The local police had promised to deploy a cruiser to patrol Windemere Drive and Valentine Pond Road.

First thing in the morning Nick was personally going to put Valerie on a plane home. He wouldn't let her begging eyes, her spew of words or her stubbornness distract him.

That left Gordon. And that meant putting all the evidence in irrefutable black and white.

Nick headed directly to his office. He would find the trail of money that led from Carter Stokke back to Gordon. The link was right there in the back of Nick's mind, itching like poison ivy. One more nail, that's all he needed to spike Gordon's coffin shut. As soon as he had that, he could finalize his report and send a copy to each of the Valentine Pond project investors as well as to the police and attorney general's office. And Gordon would go back behind bars where he belonged.

At his desk, Nick's determined fingers spelled out the evidence against his father, but his mind couldn't help straying to Valerie.

He'd let her get to him. She was there in his head constantly, haunting him in a way Valentina never had. How could he keep her safe when he couldn't think straight?

He raked both hands through his hair and kneaded the back of his aching neck. Then a warm sensation brushed against him. He stiffened and slowly turned in the direction of the window. As if thinking of her had conjured her up, Valerie stood outside, fist poised over his front door. His heart did a loop. As he rose, every nerve in his body sang with anticipation.

He yanked the door open, letting in the cold wind and her warm scent of ginger. "You shouldn't be out here."

She wrung her hands. "Nick, look, you got everything wrong."

"It's fine. Let me walk you back to the mansion."

"I wanted to call you, but Rita insisted I didn't. Jeez, Louise, she's an adult. She ought to be able to make her own decisions at this stage of her life."

He forced a careless shrug. "I agree."

She tilted her head and frowned. "I haven't done anything to deserve your suspicion. From the beginning, I've gone out of my way to be open and honest with you about everything regarding Valentina. You're the one who keeps shutting me out."

"I've had to protect Rita for a long time." And Rita had been the last thing on his mind when he'd roared.

Valerie blew out a breath. "That's no reason to bite someone's head off."

"It's not you. It's me." *I need you safe.* And that need made him too vulnerable. He wanted to touch her, to hold her, to lose himself in her. And that wasn't like him.

"Nick…it's okay. You're allowed to show that you care for Rita. You're human."

More than he wanted. "I can't get you out of my head." *My blood. My soul.* "Do you know what that's like? To have someone invade your mind when you know you shouldn't trust her?"

A pulse of understanding jumped in her eyes, sparking them with a flash of heat.

He wanted to shut the door on her and walk back into his logical and ordered life.

But he couldn't. She had a hold on him he couldn't

explain. The harder he tried to fight that hold, the tighter it wound around him. If he let go, if he gave in, would it set him free?

She pressed one hand flat against her belly. "I should go."

"That would be best." His voice was harsh, like ice cracking.

She turned to leave, and the sense of looming horror returned, clawing his chest wide-open. He jerked her against him. What was he doing? Breathless alarm rattled deep in his bones. He didn't want her to leave. He couldn't lose her. His grip squeezed her hand tight as if she could simply slip out of his grasp.

Her fingers dug hard into his shoulders and held on. Her gaze challenged him, but in the dark mirror of her widened pupils, he saw her surrender. She sighed into him. "Nick..."

The power of that simple act of pure trust rocked through him, destroying what little control he had left. "You should leave."

"I think it's too late."

His hands slid into the loose hair that draped over her shoulder, a pale slide of light as erotic as silk on skin. Something about her invited touch, begged him to taste her. As if it had a mind of its own, his mouth came down on hers. An instant flare of need kicked him in the gut.

Her lips parted. Her body yielded. And his mind gave in to his heart's ache. "No one's going to hurt you," he whispered against her ear. "I promise."

"I'm not your responsibility."

"Valerie—"

She put a hand over his lips. "Stop analyzing. I'm starting to believe that some questions don't have answers."

She feathered her lips over his, and her tender kiss spun him dizzy.

Giving in to temptation was what he'd been avoiding all day. But distance and danger had only served to hone his desire. He kicked the door shut behind her. The heat of her small body wrapped around him. In a ballet as smooth as if they'd been partners forever, they kissed and touched and twirled down the hall to his bedroom.

Moonlight filtered through the window. Stars dusted the night sky. The soft glow of the lamp from his office warmed the shadows of the room and bathed her skin in soft gold. The spicy ginger of her scent teased him, tempted him to devour. "You're beautiful and—"

"Nick…"

His mouth frantically roamed over her face, her neck, her shoulders. "I hate the way you twist me around." His impatient hands made short work of the buttons of her blouse and the zipper of her skirt. "I hate the way I want you."

"I know." Her palms spread heat across his skin like wind-fed flames.

"Tell me to stop."

"Don't stop." And like kindling, she willingly burned under his touch.

Objections formed in his throat, but came out torn apart, sparks that flamed hot and died fast. Why object when she wanted this as much as he did?

All reason, all rational thought became smoke in the night.

He wanted her. With an unexpected desperation that only fanned his need, she pulled at his shirt and tugged at his pants.

The wind stirring the clouds outside echoed the rush of their pulses. The quickening drum against the walls pounded in time to their racing heartbeats.

He lifted her into his arms, cradling her like the most fragile of Rita's crystal, then set her down on his bed. "Valerie…"

"Shh, it's okay."

Not okay. Nothing was okay. The fabric of the world he'd known was coming apart at the seams. He'd wanted her, he realized, from that first day when she'd insisted she belonged at Moongate.

He took rash pleasure from the firm stroke of her delicate fingers over his chest, the bold brush of her small palms across his hips, the relentless teasing of her lips, and returned each favor with equal fervor. She strained against him, demanding more. And when he thought she was about to flame out, he pushed inside her and set her ablaze all over again.

She gasped as if he'd touched an inner corner of her never before explored. Her eyes flew open, as blue and brilliant as the heated heart of a flame, and locked into his gaze, pupils wide and deep, inviting him in.

Her hands came up to frame his jaw. "I've been looking for you all of my life."

Chapter Thirteen

Valerie's words shattered through Nick. They shook through his release, nearly tearing him apart. She arched under him, melting into him, her arms locking him to her.

The roaring in his head matched the fierce hammer of his heart. Valerie's unsteady breaths pulsed against his neck as he hung on to her, afraid to let her go, afraid to let her see the wildfire of emotions she'd ignited. Furnace-hot, his breath burned into his lungs.

What had he done? How could she make him feel so much in so little time? He'd been so careful, kept himself under such tight control.

Unnerved by his weakness, he rolled onto his side, reluctantly breaking the snug bond of her arms. She rolled with him, then looked up at him, reaching a hand toward his. "Hey, where are you going?"

God, her smile. It dazzled with pure joy and unadulterated hunger, and blazed inside him like a sun. He hadn't felt so desired, so wanted, so needed in a long time.

A shock jolted through his system. It couldn't be true, he couldn't love her. But he did.

How could he have fallen for her? It had all happened too fast, too hard. But even as he fought the unworldly strength of this *thing* raging through him, he bent down to kiss the top of her head as if nothing had happened between them. That small taste of her yielding warmth punched through his system, resparking a desire that should have died to coals by now.

And just the thought of so much need frightened him.

He started to push away, but her hand shackled his wrist.

She frowned. "You're angry? About this?"

"I have work to do."

"Not tonight, you don't." She tilted her head in that way that made him feel as if she could read him too clearly. "This—"

"Was really nice, but I'm not good at the morning-after goodbyes." He ripped his gaze from her eyes to avoid seeing the hurt he'd placed there. It was for her own good, he reminded himself. To keep her safe.

"So you're just going to go hide until I disappear?"

He winced at her choice of words. "It's for the best."

Her grip on his wrist tightened. "I don't date much. Not with the hours my job demands. And this—wow—I've never felt like this before. And I know you felt something, too."

With a smile tipped with an intriguing mix of promise and vulnerability, she pulled him back down to her. "Running won't make it go away."

Cursing under his breath, he fell into her arms once more—the first place that had felt right in a long while. "Moongate is dangerous for you."

"I'm safe right here." Her smile bloomed again as she snuggled closer to him.

A caustic stew of longing and dread bubbled in his gut. "In the morning, you have to leave."

She shrugged. "In the morning, we'll see."

"Cripes, you don't take no for an answer, do you?"

She kissed the hot pulse at his neck. "No."

A few more hours. What harm could it do? It wasn't as if he could stuff her in a plane right this minute. At least by his side, he'd know where she was.

As he held her tight, he traced the scythe of scar along her right temple, wanting to erase anything that could have ever hurt her. "Where did you get that?"

"I don't remember. My mother says it happened when I was three, when I went down a slide headfirst and too fast and landed on a rock."

Why hadn't her mother been there to catch her and keep her safe? He could have lost her tonight. Whoever had attacked her could have taken her and hurt her. What if he couldn't protect her even if she returned safely home?

Her hand skimmed his chest and came to rest over his heart. Laughing softly, she burrowed her head in the crook of his shoulder. "Stop analyzing, Nick. We're not a stock. We just are."

Her hand roamed the plane of his chest. His whole body sighed with a frightening contentment. She rolled on top of him, her blue eyes aglow. Flesh connected with flesh, from chest to toe, but it wasn't enough. He wanted something more, something just out of reach. The echo of a ghost pain, a soft mourning for the something he couldn't name keened in his chest.

As he slid into her once again, he realized that he'd fallen for the one woman who would forever remind him of his failure.

And in the morning, he would have to let her go.

VALERIE WOKE UP to the pale gray light of a rain-soaked morning filtering through the window and spilling on the disarray of sheets around her, and not an ounce of her usual shame flip-flopped through her mind. Never had everything in the world felt so good, so beautiful, so right, and she wanted to hold on to this amazing feeling for as long as she could.

To add to her sense of heaven, the scent of coffee drifted in from the hallway. Wearing only black track pants low on his hips, Nick appeared, a tall latte mug in hand. "Big enough?"

A smile ran away from her as she sat up and accepted the mug with just the right amount of cream. He looked good mussed from sleep. Nothing starched about him at all at the crack of dawn. "Definitely."

He squeezed in next to her and put an arm around her shoulders. Content, she thought. Like a spring day at the beach—warm, relaxed, comfortable. And she wanted to stay right here and bask in that contentment forever. But Higgins expected his package and she had an interview with Hillary Clark this morning. She'd known from the start this was a stolen night, hadn't she? Still, what harm would it do to linger over coffee?

Nick rubbed the knuckles of her free hand with his thumb. The longing in his dark eyes was so raw that it turned the air to pure static electricity. Would he think her too bold if she kissed him and reignited the fire that had burned so hot between them?

He leaned his head against hers. "I've made a reservation for you on the ten o'clock flight."

So much for a day at the beach. "I have an eleven o'clock interview."

"You'll have to cancel."

More than the logistics of miles, families and careers separated them. Valentina was a mountain as big as Mount Monadnock standing right between them. What if they never found her? Could she live in the constant shadow of a ghost? "I really like you, Nick, and I want the chance to find out where this relationship could go. That can't happen until we find Valentina. So I'm not quitting until we do."

As if Valerie had zapped him with a live wire, he whipped his legs over the side and sat on the edge of the bed, raking a hand through his hair and shaking his head. "She's been gone twenty-five years. Do you really think you can do anything to change that?"

Suddenly cold, she reached for the sheet and tucked it over her exposed breasts, then wrapped both hands around the mug and hunched over the steaming coffee. "Yes. The fact that someone tried to scare me away yesterday says we're getting close to the truth." Over the top of her cup, she glanced at Nick's bowed head. "I think you know more than you're telling me."

In his memories—that's where they'd find the answers.

He threw her a sharp look over his shoulder. "Talking won't help."

His combative tone and rigid posture were erecting a barrier between them. Pulse pounding in a mad zigzag, Valerie tiptoed along that craggy ledge, dizzy with the knowledge that every word could pitch her off the last inch of that secure shelf. She didn't want to risk losing him, but without answers, she didn't have him anyway.

"It's not the talking you're afraid of." She kept her voice soft and even. "It's the old emotions it'll bring up." Emotions far too big for one little boy to handle.

"And you know that how?"

She tucked a strand of snarled hair behind her ear. "I once did a segment on a psychologist who specialized in memory."

"So that makes you an expert?"

"It makes me someone who's willing to listen." Was he afraid of judgment? Afraid she would think less of him for his perceived failure? To her dismay, the chasm of that long-ago night was already growing between them as if what they'd shared on this night had never happened, as if the space of peace they'd found was nothing but a pause while the ghost between them solidified its shape.

"Memories can be frightening." Valerie clutched her coffee cup, bracing against the bruise of his distance throbbing through her whole body. "Even the ones we make up. I've had a recurring nightmare of being chased in some dark swamp since I was a kid. It comes every time I'm under stress. But when I face it, when I label it, the fear fades."

His gaze cut through the window and across the lawn

to the blurry gray shape of the mansion, shrouded in rain—then kept going, sliding into a past only he could see.

Face grimly set, he sat unmoving, breath practically stopped, back muscles hard as granite against her thigh. "I saw the man who took her away. I just lay curled up, frozen."

Her heart bled for him. He'd carried a burden much to heavy for a child. "Your silence kept you alive. Would Rita have felt better if you'd been kidnapped, too?"

"I could've done *something*—cried, yelled, run for help. But I just lay there." His voice was so flat that it made her blood run cold.

And he'd been blaming himself ever since.

She set the mug on the night table, wrapped her arms around his waist and laid her cheek against his shoulder. "You were scared."

"So was she." His breath choked. "She was the one person who loved me without reservation, and I let her be taken away without doing anything to help her."

In the muscle-memory of fright quivering through his body, the answering echo of Valentina's fear rippled through Valerie. *Nick, Nick, Nick.* Valerie shook away the old film whirring to life. Nick needed her to stay focused on him.

He tried to shrug out of her arms, but she refused to let go. "And you've spent your life looking for her." If she kept on this track, he would associate her with the pain she forced him to dredge up. But he needed answers. "Close your eyes, put yourself back in the tower room on that night. He's big and dressed in black and he scoops up Valentina."

Nick exhaled in a ragged burst. "When he lifts her up,

her head catches on the corner of the bureau. There's blood. A lot of blood."

"Even superficial head wounds bleed a lot." This bit came courtesy of a segment on first aid she'd done a few years ago. "She probably wasn't as hurt as you think."

"She hung from his shoulder like she was dead. Her eyes were half-closed. Her arms were limp, bumping against him."

Gently, Valerie prodded Nick. "What about the man? What did you notice about him?"

He ground the heels of his hands into his eyes. "Nothing. All I saw was Valentina."

"Can you look at your memories as if you were watching a movie? That little boy on the ground isn't you. He's just an actor. What does he see, hear, smell?"

Nick shook his head. "I can't do this."

She pressed a kiss into the stiff stone of his back. "Yes, you can. For Valentina. For Rita. For yourself. If we know who took her, then we can find her."

He swallowed hard. "I see the blood—"

Her throat went narrow at the pain in his voice. "Try it in third person. *He* sees the blood…"

"He sees Valentina. He thinks she's dead. He can't move."

"What does he see?"

"He sees her moving **away.**"

The man's hard **shoulder dug** into her stomach. Her breath stuck in **lungs that** couldn't work. Nick, under her blanket, getting **smaller** and darker and farther. *Nick, Nick, Nick. Help me.* The film ripped, clacking in the projector's mechanism. A burst of white, then black. *Nick!*

His memories, she realized, were fueling the snippets of movies Valentina insisted on etching in the valleys of her mind.

"Then what?" Valerie asked. "Did the kidnapper go out the door?"

Nick picked his words as if they were grenades that could blow apart his world. "He stopped at the door. He opened it. Light from the hallway came into the room."

"Then what?"

He slowly turned to face her. "I see his face."

Valerie noticed he wasn't speaking in the third person anymore. Both her hands squeezed one of his. "Describe him."

Nick's dark eyes took on a haunted look. "His eyes."

Breath gushed out of her. "You remember."

Nick buried his head in his free hand. "It can't be. It just can't be."

"Can't be what? Who do you see?"

Nick drew in a shaky breath. "We were both on the floor, sleeping under blankets. He took her. He just took her like she was nothing. I want to call out, but I'm afraid that he'll take me, too. And I don't want to go with him. He'll hurt me. Just like he'll hurt her."

"Who?"

Pain carved Nick's face as he turned to look at her. "My father."

His father. Oh, God, no. Hot tears coursed down her

cheeks. How could a father do this to his son? How could a son endure such betrayal? "It wasn't your fault. You were scared."

His voice rode a flat line becoming all but dead. "All these years, I've been protecting my own damn father."

"No, all these years you were protecting yourself from a betrayal so painful your mind shut it out. We have to call the police. Let them know. They can pick him up and question him. Then you'll have your answers."

He stood so fast, her hands ached as if they were bandages he'd ripped off his skin. "No, I'm going to handle this my own way. You have to leave. *Now.*"

Frowning, she shook her head. "I'm not going to leave you. Not like this."

"You don't have a choice. I know what my father's like. He attacked you last night, and he's going to use you to get to Rita, to get to me."

Heat rose up her neck. "How? He's not magic. He can't get through the layers of security you've installed. The cops are already looking for him for the real estate scam."

"You don't know him."

"I can't leave. This is my job."

"He's a vicious man when he thinks he's been wronged. He's already tried to hurt you. He's threatened your mother. I can't risk you. I won't risk you."

"It's not your decision." She fashioned the sheet into a toga and swung her legs over the edge of the bed.

He leaned into her, fists dipping the mattress on both sides of her, caging her. "If I have to put you on that plane kicking and screaming, you're leaving. This morning."

"Are you hearing yourself?" She reached for Nick, but he moved away.

"Memories are painted with emotions. The stronger the emotion, the deeper the groove, the sharper the memory. Your father betrayed you, so you buried the wound. Now that you've allowed yourself to see it, your whole body and soul tells you it's true. And that scares you as much as not knowing. Because now you have to do something about it. I'll help you. I need to help you."

"Don't you get it? You look too much like Valentina. I can't—" His gaze slid around the room, avoiding hers.

She got it. She finally got it. Even if they found Valentina's body, Valerie would always be a painful reminder of his failure.

Lightning whipped fire through the sky and thunder roared, echoing the scream clawing and snarling inside her. The sky shed the tears she refused to turn loose. Understanding the reason for his rejection didn't make it any easier to take.

Fingers at her throat, she snatched a breath to say something else, then thought better of it. She was the one who'd insisted he tear away the veil to his nightmare. She'd known the risk. Now she had to live with the consequence. Swaddled in her mock toga, she plucked her clothes along the way to the bathroom.

He followed her and stopped the door before she could shut it all the way. The light in his eyes burned hard as if embers were locked in his pupils. "Valerie... I'm sorry..."

He dropped his chin to his chest, then slowly raised it

again. A growl erupted from deep in his throat. Lightning fractured the silence, haloing him with light, and thunder ripped through the sky, rattling the windows. "I never wanted to hurt you."

A gasp of cold air cut her to the bone. "Yeah, can't risk letting anyone get too close to you."

"Be ready to go in an hour." Without waiting for a response, he disappeared into the shadows of his office, slamming the door behind him.

As if she were viewing an old movie, black-and-white and sharp with shadows, she followed his rigid path, fully expecting The End to pop up on the black screen of his closed door. Her arms lashed over her chest to keep herself from coming apart.

BACK IN HER ROOM at the mansion, Valerie started to pack. But a wisp of Valentina's memory kept nagging at her. A picture of trees and water and a boulder shaped like a heart tumbled on its side. What if that was where Nick's father had buried Valentina?

Between the security system with all its intruder-warning gadgets, the extra police patrols and Lionel watching the closed-circuit television screens, no one could get on to the estate without triggering some sort of alarm. The power was back on, so everything was up and running—not like last night when the wind had cut holes into the defenses.

And she had to keep moving or the toxins of her rising anxiety would burst like a dam. She'd bawl and she didn't want Nick to see how much he'd hurt her when he came looking for her—not that she had any intentions of running back home without solving the last piece of this puzzle. Besides, if she could find Valentina's grave, then maybe he could heal. That gave her hope for both of them.

She changed into her running gear, then set out for the pond trail. She was sure she'd seen the lopsided heart-shaped rock along there on a previous run.

She'd handled Nick all wrong, she decided as she found her rhythm. She should have been less pushy. He was right. She wasn't an expert. A willingness to listen wasn't enough. Not when the territory of memories was so fraught with land mines. What had made her think she could give him the answers he needed when she couldn't find her own?

She lengthened her stride until her lungs screamed. At least he had the truth—or part of it anyway.

The sky was the color of granite and so low its weight pressed against her shoulders. In the diffuse light, she wasn't sure what time it was. The smell of winter was metallic in the air, but the air was warm and she unzipped her jersey hoodie.

Her feelings for Nick were skewing her professional ethics. How could she present a balanced story when she herself teetered on the edge of an emotional cliff? Maybe it was time to admit that another producer would do a better job of this story, that she wasn't ready to move up to harder-hitting news.

Her objectivity was warped beyond recognition. And for what? They'd come together like fire and wood, but fires that hot-burned to ashes in no time. What had she expected?

Love was more than the fast flame of passion. Love took time. Love took friendship, understanding and sharing.

Love took trust.

And she wanted Nick to trust her, to believe her, to know without a doubt that she would stand by him no matter what.

She would find Valentina, she vowed as she scoured the path for the heart-shaped boulder, and she would give him an end to this chapter of his life.

Something on the narrow road crunched on the other side of Moongate's stone wall, tires grinding on gravel, making an awful sound like the shattering of brittle bones.

Nick? Too early yet to talk to him. They both needed to cool down, sort things through. That's why he'd given her an hour. Probably just the police on their extra patrol.

Foiling her best effort to squash the memory, last night's attack rose to her mind anyway and a trill of panic quaked through her chest. What if Nick was right and his father could get through all the estate's defenses? Better head back. She'd look for the boulder when the mist wasn't so thick. She scrunched her head down and plunged into the foot trail that would lead back to the mansion.

Through the trees, the sinking fog smudged the contours of the mansion and another turn soon enveloped her in her own world. She pushed herself faster along the path. Two more minutes and she'd be safely inside.

She huffed out a breath and shook her head. "Listen to yourself. Noises echo in the fog. Duh, normal. You're always imagining the worst."

She veered toward the gazebo.

A tingly sensation rippled along the back of her neck as if someone was breathing on her. Her steps slowed. Her hearing tuned in to the sounds around her.

A gurgle of water whispered against the reeds flanking the pond. Her even footsteps squished against the rain-soaked ground of the path, lifting pockets of peaty scent. Her lungs puffed in regular spurts, melding her smoky breath with the fog. The slip of jersey against jersey swished as she pumped her arms.

The mansion was just ahead. She stepped onto the blue-stone walkway. Up ahead were the steps that led to the patio and back entrance. Almost there.

Just as relief sighed through her, electric eels of pain exploded through her head, knocking her off her feet. Agony burrowed deep into her eyes, scorching her brain and the last words she heard before everything went black were, "You didn't listen. You were always too stubborn for your own good."

Chapter Fourteen

Elbows on his desk, face buried in his hands, Nick listened to the lash of Valerie's clothes as she hurried to dress, to the uneven tattoo of her steps as she darted down the oak floor of the hallway.

Taking what she'd offered selflessly last night had been greedy. But he hadn't been able to let her go. Twenty-five years of feeling nothing but guilt and obligation, and Valerie's compassion had cracked his protective armor in a hundred pieces. Cripes, he loved her, but he had a terrible feeling that loving her was a way to ease the guilt that would never end.

Wounding Valerie, turning away from her as if she meant nothing had hurt like hell. With her here, he couldn't concentrate on catching Gordon. Away from Moongate, Valerie would be safe, and the bruise he'd had to inflict would soon heal.

The phone on his desk rang just as the front door closed. His heart leaped as he watched Valerie disappear down the driveway back to the mansion. He missed her already.

Be a man, Nick. Let her go. You can do this.

He knuckled his chest, but the deep ache wouldn't go away. He closed his eyes and concentrated on the voice on the other end of the line. "Joe, tell me you have good news."

"Nick, I have good news." Joe paused for effect. The man loved drama. "I've found Valentina."

Nick stood up so fast his office chair rolled backward and cracked against the wall. "Where?"

"Remember how I told you there was something I wanted to check out?"

Nick squeezed the receiver. "Joe, I'm really not in a patient mood right now. Get to the point."

"I went to Melbourne where Valerie was born, and I checked out her birth certificate. Valerie Grace Zea was born May 13, the same year as Valentina."

"So she's not Valentina." He'd already figured as much from the information Joe had already provided him.

"Since you were so adamant about her first breath, I asked around at the hospital and in the old neighborhood."

Nick clutched the back of his neck. "Is this going somewhere?"

"Give me a second." Joe's pen clicked in time to his rapid-fire speech. "Valerie Grace Zea was born with a congenital heart disease. She died forty-nine months later."

Nick stopped breathing. "Died?"

"As in buried. I saw the death certificate. I visited the grave. Heart failure. The family moved to Orlando four months later. When they moved into the house, they arrived with a four-year-old little girl. Care to guess what month they closed on that house?"

"October." Like a deflated balloon, Nick fell into his

chair. After all of these years of looking for her, she'd come to him and he'd pushed her away.

"Close. November," Joe said. "Heard from my lab guy, by the way. The DNA is a match. Valerie Zea is Valentina Callahan."

Valerie was Valentina. Valentina was alive. Valentina was here. His flood of joy at the news stopped cold and fear as he'd never known iced his blood. "I have to go."

"I'll mail you a copy of everything I found. And my bill, of course."

"Yeah." But Nick heard nothing over the whoosh of blood pounding over his ear.

Valentina was alive. She was here. She was Valerie. How could he have let her out of his sight?

He shot into the hall, only to realize he wore nothing but track pants. He detoured to his bedroom, tugged on a pair of jeans and a sweater, then shoved his feet into sneakers. Running at full speed, he barreled through the mansion's front door in record time. Mike's rental was still parked outside. Valerie hadn't yet fled from his unconscionable act of cruelty.

He took the stairs by threes and pounded on her door with his fist. "Valerie!"

No answer.

Forget politeness. There was no time for that. He shoved the door open.

The room was still and silent, a page from a decorating magazine. Her bag was packed and ready to go, but she was nowhere in sight. He crossed to the bathroom that smelled of her ginger shampoo and soap. The clothes she'd worn yesterday were balled in a corner, thrown there as if she never planned on wearing them again.

He swore. He'd done that to her. How could he have been such a jackass?

Last night was the best night of his life, and he'd pushed her away. "Valerie!"

No answer, but the creaks and cracks of an old house.

Nick raced back down the stairs and into the dining room, where he found Mike text messaging on his cell phone in between bites of pancakes, but not Valerie.

"Have you seen Valerie?" Nick asked, already poised for flight.

"Not since yesterday." Mike glanced at the mantel clock on the sideboard. "She's late, too. We need to leave soon if we're going to make the interview, and I have a stop to make first."

"If you see her, keep her here until I talk to her. It's very important I talk to her."

Mike blinked. "Sure, man, don't have a cow."

Nick tore down the hallway and nearly plowed into Gardner, coming out of the kitchen.

"Have you seen Valerie?"

Gardner frowned. "I thought I saw her go out a little while ago."

Out? "Which way did she go?"

Gardner pointed toward the pond.

The pond! How could she do this? How could she go there after her attack last night? He crashed through the kitchen and out the back door, leaving his mother shouting after him.

"Valerie!" Muffled by the rising fog, his own voice came back at him.

He pounded down the bluestone steps. A slash of something on the ground caught his eye. A piece of cloth the color of crushed berries. He twisted his sore knee as he veered off the path and lifted the material off the ground. A zippered hoodie, the kind joggers wore.

Valerie's.

A dark, oily kind of fear welled. The look of heartbreak on Valerie's face could not be his last image of her.

He hugged the jacket to his chest, inhaling Valerie's spicy scent. *God, no. Let her be safe.*

He could not lose her a second time.

Lionel tromped around the bend of the house and hooked a thumb over his shoulder. "There's a courier at the gate. Says he has a package you have to sign."

"Sign it yourself." Nick scoured the ground where he'd found Valerie's jacket and spotted two sets of footprints in the mud. He was too late. How could that be? The security system. The cameras. The police patrols. He'd know if anyone had breached the estate.

"He says it has to be you," Lionel grumbled. "He has to wait for an answer."

A sick feeling wormed through Nick's gut. He was too late. The thrash of mud, the discarded jacket, the awful keening in his gut said it all. Valerie was already gone and the courier was bringing proof.

Throat tight, Nick sent Lionel to call the police while he went to the gate. On the other side of the locked gate, a teenager waited, tapping a manila envelope against the hood of his truck to the thump of rap blasting from the speakers.

"You Galloway?" the kid asked, the loose layers of his clothes making him look bulkier than he was.

Nick nodded. The kid shoved the envelope at him. "I'm supposed to wait for a bag."

"Got a knife?"

The kid pulled out a penknife from his loose-fitting jeans. Nick slit the envelope and, tugging only on one corner, pulled out the paper inside. He slipped the penknife in his own pocket.

"One million in cash and you get Valentina back," the note read. "Use the ready-bag. In three hours, she'll run out of air."

The cutout letters reminded him of the ones on the note Rita had received twenty-five years ago. How did Gordon know about the duffel in the safe—stashed with twenties, just in case the kidnapper ever made a second demand?

"Who gave you this?" Nick's voice boomed, loud and impatient.

The kid shrugged. "Some guy."

"What guy?"

The kid lowered the bill of his red baseball cap. "How should I know?"

Nick fought the urge to strangle the kid. "What did he look like?"

"I don't know. Big. Dark hair. Green eyes. Friendly looking."

Definitely Gordon.

Nick swore.

The kid backed up. "He gave me five Jacksons and told

me to make sure you got the envelope, then bring back the bag. That's all I know. I swear."

"Bring it back to where?" Gordon couldn't be stupid enough to think that Nick would just hand over the bag.

"The Mobil station outside of town. The one with the red kayak on the roof."

Fighting for calm, Nick turned to Lionel who puffed out that the cops were on their way. "Don't let this punk go anywhere."

Fury made him dizzy. Where had Gordon taken Valerie? How much time did she have left?

PRESSURE BUILT LIKE STEAM as Nick returned to the mansion, but he couldn't let it vent. He had to stay in control. He had to think logically. He had to find Valerie before Gordon followed through on his threat to let her suffocate.

The cops were checking out the gas station, but Nick knew they'd find nothing there. The ruse was a classic Three-Card Monte where the quick hand distracted the eye. Gordon wanted Nick to lose track of the upper card.

Not going to work, Dad.

He'd taken his eye off the mark once. He wasn't going to make the same mistake twice.

When he didn't find his mother in the kitchen, Nick headed to Rita's room.

Though Rita had hired his mother as a housekeeper soon after Nick's birth, Rita had treated her like a friend and confidante. When Gordon's get-rich-quick schemes and his volatile temper had threatened his family's security, Rita had promised shelter and help to Holly. With that safety net, Holly had found the courage to divorce Gordon. His mother had gained full custody when his father had failed to appear for the hearing. In a show of loyalty to his mother, Nick had legally changed his name to adopt hers.

But all of their successes at carving out a solid life had festered like poisoned thorns in Gordon's side. And he was back to make them pay.

At the door to Rita's room, Nick signaled his mother, then waited for her in Rita's dove-gray sitting room, pacing like a mustang in a corral.

"How's Rita doing?" he asked when his mother came in.

Brows pinched, she shook her head. "The fever's back. I have a call in to Dr. Marzan."

Rita had to get through this. She had to know she was right. He had to give her Valentina. It was the least he could do. He took his mother by both arms and sat her down in the gray floral brocade armchair.

"Mom." His voice broke like a teenager's as he crouched in front of her. "You have to help me."

"What's wrong, Nicky?"

"Valerie…" His throat tightened and he shook his head to release his voice. "She's Valentina."

Holly's eyes widened and she shook her head in quick, short strokes. "No, Nicky, that's not possible."

"Joe found her. A couple in Florida raised her."

Holly's mouth gaped open. "No…"

"I remembered, Mom. I saw him. Gordon stole her."

She placed a hand against his jaw. "No, Nicky, no. He would have hurt me before he'd steal a child."

"The DNA matches."

His mother's face went sheet-pale, and she shrank away from him. "I thought she was one of them."

"So did I." And he'd treated Valerie like the rest of the pseudo-Valentinas who'd come knocking at the door, looking for an easy payout.

Holly's fingers knitted tightly together. "Nicky, I never meant to hurt her."

"What do you mean?"

Holly's gaze dropped to her lap. "I wanted her to leave us alone. Rita, she's gone through so much. I couldn't bear to see her hurt again."

"Mom? What did you do?"

Holly looked up, eyes drooping with regret, tears magnifying her dark eyes. "I sprinkled her food with mouse poison."

Nick shot up. "You what!"

Holly inched herself out of the chair. "Not enough to kill her. Just enough to make her sick." She hugged herself. "I thought…I thought she would go. That things could go back to normal."

Valerie's constant acid stomach. He'd assumed it was from the gallons of coffee she drank. He grasped his mother's shoulders. "How much, Mom?"

"A few flakes, that's all." She gulped. "With every meal."

What were the effects? Had the poison weakened her enough to make her easy prey for Gordon? Would it make her run out of air sooner? Nick had to find her.

He swallowed a roar and forced his voice to remain even. "Mom, listen, this is important. Do you remember any of the places Gordon used to hang around when he lived here?"

Holly's shoulders sagged. "It was so long ago—"

He shook Holly slightly. "He's back, Mom. And he has her. I have to find him before he hurts her."

Holly crossed both hands over her heart. "Oh, Nicky, no. Not again."

"Think, Mom. Where could he have taken her?"

VALERIE AWOKE in a dark so deep she couldn't see her own nose. Her head ached in a pulsing drumbeat. Her skin crawled with ripples of ice. And her chest already tingled with needles of stark terror. Any second now full-blown panic would explode and swallow her whole.

Stay calm. You're okay. A little dark never killed anyone.

Where was she? She tried to lift her arm to read her watch, but something wedged her shoulders in tight.

Shivers skittered along her skin as she remembered the attack, felt the knot of blood-matted hair, sticky against her skull. He'd knocked her out? Where had he put her? In a car trunk? No, she wasn't moving. In a closet? A powerful need to cry shook through her.

Breathe. Just breathe.

Hand shaking, she reached for the cell phone in the zippered pocket of her jogging pants. In the tight space, she managed to inch the phone up her body and flip it open.

The light from the screen glowed an eerie blue, lighting her surroundings.

Blood leached out of her veins.

She was in a coffin, buried alive.

Chapter Fifteen

"Help!" The word caught in Valerie's throat like a blade, bleeding her raw. She kept screaming, her voice climbing a rope of hysteria. A thousand terrified thoughts scrambled like panicked mice gnashing through her mind. She couldn't stop or the silence would get her. God, the silence. So deep. So empty. On top of the darkness, it was too much. "Help, someone, help me!"

Don't panic. Save your breath. Panic increased the heart rate and that led to fast breathing, which used up the oxygen faster. Where had she heard that?

Don't panic. Do something.

Her fingers worked the buttons of her cell phone, but it kept insisting she had no service.

She was completely alone.

Terror rose again, threatening to consume her.

Don't panic. You can't panic.

How long before she ran out of air?

She didn't want to die. How could she die now when she hadn't even done a quarter of the things on her life plan? She hadn't trekked across Europe. She hadn't learned to fly so she could take off for weekends in the Bahamas. She hadn't ridden across the Andes.

She hadn't told Nick she loved him.

Even if he could never love her because she looked like Valentina, she wanted him to know that she loved him and wouldn't expect him to forget about his first companion.

She wasn't thirty yet. Too young to die.

"You can't just lie here and wait to die." She fought to slow her petrified breaths. "You have to come up with a plan."

NICK JUMPED INTO HIS CAR. The revving growl of the engine as he slammed the pedal didn't come close to the howl in his brain. Rain had started again as a cold front pushed through. Where was Valerie? Was she out there cold and wet? Scared? Dead?

No, he refused to believe that. He was *not* going to lose her twice.

He swallowed over the sudden lump in his throat. He could not imagine living without her. How had she become so important so quickly? Had some part of him known all along that she was Valentina?

This could not be happening. He couldn't have found her just to lose her again. He wouldn't give up. Valerie couldn't be dead. She *wasn't* dead. He would find her.

The police cruiser sitting at the end of Windemere Drive slowed him down. Good, they were already canvassing the neighborhood for information on Valerie and Gordon. Nick would have to write a note to the department commending them on such fast action. An officer stood while an Ichabod Crane-like man windmilled his arms. For a second Nick thought he was part of the gaudy Halloween display.

Nick braked, rolled down the window and called to the officer. "Find anything yet?"

"Not a clue." The man's voice rose with each word. "How can someone just take a coffin like that? It's not exactly easy to drag around."

"A coffin?"

"For the mummy. It was here last night when we got home from dinner out. And it was gone this morning when I went out to get the paper."

"Nothing else was taken or disturbed?" the officer asked.

The man plucked the fallen mummy and lifted it back into position. "No, just the coffin. Halloween's coming. Damn high school kids probably stole it for a prank."

A rabid sickness twisted Nick's gut. *In three hours, she'll run out of air.* Gordon had stolen the coffin. He'd buried Valerie in it.

God, no. That was too horrible to even think about.

Urgency zapped his every nerve as he shoved the car into gear. "Gordon Archer stole the coffin. He's kidnapped Valerie Zea and put her in it. Spread the word. We have to find her!"

"Sir—"

Nick rammed the gas pedal and the car lurched forward. He had to find Valerie. Fast.

Dark clouds, laden with rain, rushed toward him—an anvil of black crushing the gray. Rain pounded down in opaque sheets. The frantic wipers gave him only a fractured glance at the road. In this weather, Gordon wouldn't have gone far. Not to Harrisville as his mother thought, to her father's old fishing cabin.

Where had Gordon gone? How much of a head start did he have? An hour? No, it had to be less. Even if he'd set the note up ahead of time and predug the grave, he'd still have had to grab Valerie and—Nick winced—bury her. Knowing Gordon he'd try to make a statement. He'd have stayed close by to drive home his point and still make a clean getaway.

And his latest failure had come at Nick's hands. He'd want to stick the point.

Nick swore.

The house. The one Gordon had used for his latest scam.

Nick cranked the wheel and risked a U-turn in the middle of 101. A semi flashed its beams and honked behind him, but Nick pressed on. With one hand, he placed a call to the police. How long ago had Gordon buried Valerie? How much of that three hours was left? She'd left his house at seven. He'd gone looking for her forty-five minutes later. The clock on the dashboard glared an ugly 10:15.

Half swearing, half praying, he hooked a left on Valentine Pond Road and nearly skidded off the gravel road. He couldn't be too late. He wouldn't let it be too late. Two hundred yards in, a hollow pine had fallen across the road, blocking his path.

Abandoning the car, he hiked over the tree. Mud and loose pebbles made for unstable footing, rain clouded his vision, but he trekked on, covering the half mile to Gordon's project as fast as he could.

Only a strand of woods separated Nick from the darkened skeleton of a house. He struck into the trees, making his way across narrow pathways that wound around him in a mesh-tight maze. Cripes, he could barely see two feet in front of him.

Shadows, everywhere in the unnatural darkness of the storm, deceived him with their sly movements. *Hang on, Valerie. I'm coming for you.*

Slipping and sliding on the fresh mud and rotting leaves, he fell hard to his knees, wasting precious time. "Valerie!"

The shout tore out of him before he could stop it. A string of bullets whizzed by him, plunking chunks of bark out of the trees around him. He dropped fast and hard, knocking his teeth into his tongue, the copper taste of blood gushing into his mouth. He rolled into a snarl of brush, heart stampeding like a runaway horse. He stayed low until his breath caught up with him.

When no more bullets chased after him, he rose and warily used the trunk of an oak for cover. Even the fall of rain hushed in the sudden, eerie quiet. The peaty scent of earth and dead leaves rose to burn his nostrils. And now that he was still, the wetness of his clothes seeped into his bones, chilling him.

He stepped from tree to tree until he reached the edge of the woods. The slap of wet footsteps on mud echoed to his right. He whipped his head around to catch Gordon hurrying toward a black utility van.

Nick gave chase. He wouldn't be able to catch the van once Gordon had it in motion. The fallen tree would stop the vehicle, but by then it would be too late for Valerie.

HER HEAD HURT. Her mouth was dry. Valerie remembered the crunch of tires. A car. The attack just as she reached the stairs leading up to the deck. How long had she been unconscious? Where had her attacker driven her to? How long had she been in here?

How long before she ran out of air?

Nick had said he was giving her an hour. Had he come looking for her? Did he know she was missing? Did *anyone*?

Find me, Nick. Please.

The light of her cell phone blinked out. The battery was dead. She'd never recharged it last night.

A scream hovered in her mouth and tears ran free. The darkness went on and on without end.

Don't panic. Conserve your air.

She whispered a rosary. She bartered with God. Still the panic snaked through her stomach, banded across her chest and cinched her throat. A red flare went off in her head.

She was dying. Right here. Right now.

Just like before.

The realization brought a surprising calm.

Against the velvet black of her tomb, a string of memories, like pearls on a broken necklace, spilled one by one.

The voice. *You're too stubborn for your own good.* Hard. Cold. She moaned. Like the one in her nightmare.

So clear now, everything.

All the lies that had woven the tight fabric of her life suddenly unraveled. Why her father had always called her Gracie. Why her mother couldn't explain why Valerie's hair had lightened with age rather than darkened. Why the removal of the mole next to her left ear had left no scar.

Her mother had once told her that the way Valerie sank her teeth into research like a wild animal frightened her. Had she been afraid Valerie would uncover the truth? That some random scrap of information could give away her secret and tear apart the careful illusion her mother worked so hard to hammer into reality?

And now that Valerie had the truth, what was she supposed to do with it?

In the dark, she had no sense of passing time. But the voice of survival screamed through her brain. She would not die here in the dark, a bug swept under the carpet to be forgotten.

She had to get out. She couldn't die. She had to tell Nick that it wasn't his fault.

NICK CLOSED THE GAP between him and Gordon. Gordon whipped around training his weapon at Nick. "Stop, boy, or I'll shoot."

He'd do it, too. No doubt about it.

"What did you do with Valerie?"

"I put her to rest." Gordon's finger tightened around the trigger of his pistol.

Nick launched himself sideways, but the expected detonation never came.

Gordon kept hammering at the trigger, but when he saw Nick advancing toward him, he pitched the useless weapon away and reached for the shovel propped against the van.

With a well-timed swipe of his arm, Nick knocked the shovel aside. He grasped the lapels of his father's shirt, heaved him off his feet and slammed him against the side of the van. He wanted to strangle him. He wanted to beat the truth out of him. "What did you do with her?"

Gordon cackled in a rising gleeful madness. "It's too late."

Nick's hands clamped tighter against Gordon's neck. "Where is she?"

"How does it feel to know you're helpless?" Gordon taunted.

"You sick bastard."

"I want you to know what it feels like."

"What's Valerie ever done to you?"

"Not her." Gordon spit a wad of blood. "That bitch Rita. She could never mind her own business. Ever since your mother started working for her, she's been poisoning Holly's mind."

Personal responsibility wasn't part of Gordon's makeup. "Mom had to work because you couldn't hold down a job."

"Rita interfered with every damn thing. It was like being married to my mother. I had brains and skills. It was just a matter of time. But could she be patient? No, she had to go crying to Rita, and Rita pushed her into divorcing me."

Nick banged his father's head against the car. "Do you think I was deaf? I heard the way you talked to your wife.

I heard her begging. I heard you hurt her, then tell her it was her own damn fault. What kind of man takes out his failure on a woman?"

Gordon's green eyes gleamed with fevered bitterness. "You were mine. She had no right to take you away from me."

"I wouldn't have gone with you even if a judge had ordered me to."

Gordon's face twisted into a sneer. "It was supposed to be you."

"What?"

"That night. I'd gone to the house for you. I was going to steal you from Holly the way she'd stolen you from me, but you were both sacked out on the floor. I grabbed the kid under the blue blanket." He snorted. "Wrong kid."

Gordon's words were a slap, and a red haze of fury blurred Nick's vision. "So you decided to ransom her."

Ever the con man, Gordon shrugged. "Why waste a good opportunity? I thought it was fitting that Rita should feel my pain since she's the one who caused it in the first place. She took my wife and my kid away from me."

"And you took her husband and her daughter."

Gordon shook his head. "Rushton took his own life. I had nothing to do with that."

"What made you think you could raise me when you couldn't make enough money to buy groceries for one?"

"I wasn't." Gordon's eyes shone bright, enjoying the torture he was inflicting. "My cousin had just lost her kid, and I was going to give you to her."

The whole puzzle fell into place.

Nick ground his teeth. "Marissa Zea is your cousin."

THE AIR WAS GETTING WARMER. Her head was swimming. It would be so easy to drift away, to close her eyes and go to sleep.

No! Stay awake!

Valerie thought back to the survival segment she'd shot, when? Just last spring?

She pressed her hands against the coffin's lid. It had some give and, according to the survival expert, that meant it would be relatively easy to break through.

What if all the earth on top of her crushed her? She should wait to be rescued. But what if rescue didn't come?

Don't think about it. Just keep moving. Step two. What was step two?

She crossed her arms over her chest and squirmed in the tight space as she pulled her long-sleeved wicking T-shirt off. Not the neat khaki safari shirt the guy had worn, but she was good at improvising. She did her best to knot the tail of her shirt to close off the opening, then slipped the shirt neck back over her head until the shirt fit like a sack.

She braced her feet against the lid. *I can't do this.*

It's do or die, Valerie, and I thought you still had things you wanted to do—like kick Nick's butt and tell him what an idiot he is for sending you away. Like telling him he can stop looking for Valentina. Like telling him you love him.

Swallowing hard, she closed her eyes and kicked at the

lid. The wood cracked, then broke apart. She screamed as loose dirt rushed in.

Stay calm. Breathe nice and slow. You can do this.

Using her hands, she pushed the dirt toward her feet. Oh, God, it was coming in too fast. She was going to drown in dirt.

In spite of the fear swimming through her muscles like spineless jellyfish, she worked at filling the space at her feet. When that space filled up, she pushed the dirt to her sides.

Her hands ached. Her fingernails tore and bled.

She kept digging.

NICK LOOKED AT HIS FATHER, the man who was supposed to have raised him, nurtured him and loved him. He looked straight into the ice-cold green eyes and swung. His fist connected with Gordon's jaw, reeling him sideways onto the hood of the van. Fists flying, Nick punched him again and again. "How does it feel to be on this side of a fist?"

"You kill me, you never find her."

Nick punched Gordon in the gut. He doubled over, staggering forward.

"Tell me where she is."

Gordon cranked his head up and looked at Nick. "You think you're so high and mighty. Just like them. But you're not. Look at yourself, boy. You're just like me."

"I'm nothing like you. I don't use the people I love. I would kill for them."

The rawness of his outburst sobered Nick. He couldn't let his temper rule. He couldn't kill this man. Gordon needed the one thing he would hate most—a public tar-and-feathering, a trial that would expose his rotten core once and for all.

With one last well-placed punch, Nick flattened Gordon. He crumpled to the ground unconscious. Nick tied Gordon up with his own belt, then raced for the house and prayed to God he'd find Valerie before she ran out of air.

VALERIE CRANKED HERSELF to a seated position. Loose earth falling into the space she'd just vacated. How deep? Sure she was going to die before she reached the top, she kept digging. She tried to ignore the plinking of the soil that kept falling around her.

She kept digging and pushing until her hand cleared the edge of the grave. Breath exploded out of her mouth. *I made it. I made it.*

Voices muted to a flannel hum penetrated through the veil of T-shirt and dirt.

Her heart stuttered and the tears came faster. She was found. Nick had found her. "Nick! Help me! Nick!"

NICK COULD FEEL HER. Somewhere close by. "Valerie!"

Where? *Please don't let it be too late.*

The sweat of terror coated his body so thickly, even the rain couldn't wash it away. "Valerie!"

He spun around, searching for evidence of her grave. How many times had she looked into his eyes, seen something he'd thought he'd hidden well and not reacted in fear?

Too much rain. Too damn much rain.

His heart knocked in his chest. Of course. Gordon wouldn't risk the rain ruining his plan.

Guided by some unknown force, Nick entered the house and scrambled down the steps leading to the basement. Gordon hadn't bothered with a concrete foundation.

In the gray murkiness of the space, Nick spotted something moving. A hand. "Valerie!"

He flung himself to the ground. Using his hands, he dug until he cleared her shoulder, then he pulled her out. She staggered like a drunk into his arms, sobbing.

He pulled off the T-shirt stuck like a sack over her head. Then he brushed dirt away from her face and hair. Blood, bruises and dirt marked her face.

"Nick." Breath tore out of her lungs. Her body shook with relief, and tears poured from her pale blue eyes. "You came."

A tidal wave of feelings old and new crashed over him. His body was ice. His brain was fire. He peppered her face with kisses, then held on to her tight. "You're alive. Thank God, you're alive."

She hiccuped a breath. "It's over."

"It's over. And I'm never going to let you go, Valentina."

She pushed away from him. "You know."

Even though his father had provided half his DNA, Nick was not his father's son. In this instant, with Valerie in his arms, Nick understood what his father never had. Success wasn't the dollars you added to your asset column, but how much love you had in your life. And Nick's portfolio was stacked with love. "I know."

Epilogue

One month later.

A stretch of fall perfection blanketed the grounds of Moongate Mansion—star-sprinkled sky, crisp moonlight and bracing wind. A dusting of the year's first snow jeweled the wide lawn and a magical trail of lanterns illuminated the driveway for the combination welcome home–belated birthday–Thanksgiving party Rita had insisted on throwing.

Luna, ensconced for the duration of the party in Nick's laundry room, yodeled at the moon, but the neighbors were too far away to care.

Valerie stopped on the drive leading from Nick's carriage house to the mansion. Her mother and Rita stood at the front door.

Rita greeted each guest with a smile and a handshake, an aura of joy gleaming around her. Her laughter chimed through the foyer in a gleeful melody.

Watching this woman who'd missed her and searched for her for twenty-five years, Valerie found it odd to know nothing about her. How could Valerie have not even known that she was missing all these years?

The answer, of course, stood next to Rita.

Her mother looked so out of place in this world of glamour, but she was trying hard to accept all the changes Valerie had wreaked by melding her past as Valentina and her present as Valerie to create a new future—one she couldn't have dreamed of when she'd written her life plan over a decade ago.

She looked at her mothers, thought of Nick and Holly, of herself, and marveled at the resiliency of the human psyche and its will to survive and thrive.

She'd grown up loved and cared for—even if smothered at times. Which made sense now that she knew her mother had lived with the terror that someone would knock on the door and claim her child.

Like it or not, Marissa Zea, even though she had not given birth to her, was her mother. She was the one who'd poured oatmeal baths when Valerie had come down with chicken pox in kindergarten. She was the one who'd fought the whole school board in middle school so her daughter would have a teacher who nurtured her spirit rather than cut it to pieces. She was the one who'd held Valerie as she'd cried her eyes out when Justin Strutton had broken her heart in ninth grade.

"Did you know?" Valerie had asked her mother when she'd gone home to explain to Higgins why the Valentina package couldn't air. "Did you know I was stolen?"

Valerie had never seen her mother so small, so cowed—so afraid. She'd sat at Valerie's kitchen table, wringing her hands until they were red and raw.

"Gordon told me your mother was a drug-addicted teenager who'd sold you to him for the price of a high. I believed him. I had no reason not to." Tears streaked down her mother's face. "He said your name was Val. I took it as a sign from heaven."

"But didn't you see the news?"

Her mother closed her eyes, pinched them tight. "I didn't turn on a television for years. No radio. No newspapers. I didn't want to accidentally read something that would make me have to give you up." She gulped in air. "I'd already lost so much."

"But something frightened you. After Dad died, you hung on to me even tighter." Valerie had thought it was because of the loss.

"When your father died, I found clippings in a safe. That's when I found out you were Valentina Callahan. Then I got scared. I didn't want to lose you. And you were working at that station—for your own great-uncle. I was so scared, Valerie. You have to forgive me."

Nick came up behind Valerie, bursting the bubble of memory. He wound his arms around her waist, and instantly her stress abated. She seemed to have grown a new skin of strength—as if her time underground had tempered her. Her hunger for information was no longer a desperate craving, but a healthy curiosity.

Though the Valentina segments hadn't aired, the story had made national news.

Gordon was charged with kidnapping and attempted murder as well as at least a dozen counts of fraud. Nick had convinced all of the Valentine Pond project investors who'd lost money to swallow their pride and testify.

As for her job, Valerie had left it in limbo for now. The good thing about nepotism was that Edmund Meadows had promised her a place should she want to return once she decided what to do with her future.

Nick kissed her temple. "How are you holding up?"

Her gaze drifted to the two women in the doorway. "I'm not sure where I fit anymore."

"Right here." He turned her in his arms and kissed her until the edges of the world softened and all her doubts disappeared and melded the person she was born with the person she'd grown into, showing her a world of possibilities.

"Wow." She pulled away from him, seeing her reflection in the dark mirror of his eyes, soft with love. She couldn't help but smile. This one truth felt right. This one truth was enough. Nick, the companion her soul had never forgotten, filled her heart with pure happiness.

Her search was over. She was home.

* * * * *

VALERIE'S FAVORITE
BIRTHDAY CAKE

3/4 cup milk
2 teaspoons instant coffee powder
3/4 cup unsweetened cocoa
1/2 cup plain yogurt
1 1/4 cups flour
1 1/2 teaspoons baking soda
1/2 teaspoon baking powder
1/4 teaspoon salt
1 cup butter, softened (no substitutions)
1 1/2 cups sugar
3 eggs
2 teaspoons vanilla

Preheat over to 350° F. Grease three 8-inch cake pans. Line bottoms with waxed paper. Grease and flour paper.

Heat milk and coffee in small saucepan until small bubbles form around the edge. Add to cocoa and whisk until smooth. Whisk in yogurt. Cool.

In medium bowl, combine flour, baking soda, baking powder and salt. Beat butter in mixer bowl until light. Gradually beat in sugar until light and fluffy. Beat in eggs one at a time. Add vanilla. At low speed, gradually beat in dry ingredients alternating with chocolate mixture. Beat at medium speed two minutes. Pour into prepared pans.

Bake 25 minutes, until tops spring back when lightly touched. Cool in pan on wire rack 10 minutes. Invert cakes onto rack. Remove paper and cool completely, right side up.

CREAMY FUDGE FROSTING

> 4 ounces unsweetened dark chocolate, chopped
> 1 2/3 cups confectioners' sugar
> 3/4 cup whipping cream
> 2 teaspoons vanilla
> 6 tablespoons butter, softened (no substitutions)

Heat chocolate, sugar and cream, stirring constantly, in saucepan over medium heat until smooth. Remove from heat; stir in vanilla. Transfer to mixer bowl, and place in larger bowl of ice water. Let stand, stirring occasionally, until cold and thick. Remove from ice bath. Gradually beat in butter at high speed; beat until fluffy and stiff enough to hold its shape.

Place one layer on cake plate and spread with 3/4 cup frosting. Top with second layer and another 3/4 cup frosting. Spread top and sides with remaining frosting.

Makes 12 servings.

*Experience entertaining women's fiction for every
woman who has wondered
"what's next?" in their lives.
Turn the page for a sneak preview of a new book from
Harlequin NEXT,
WHY IS MURDER ON THE MENU, ANYWAY?
by Stevi Mittman*

On sale December 26, wherever books are sold.

Design Tip of the Day

Ambience is everything. Imagine eating a foie gras at a luncheonette counter or a side of coleslaw at Le Cirque. It's not a matter of food but one of atmosphere. Remember that when planning your dining room design.

—Tips from *Teddi.com*

"Now that's the kind of man you should be looking for," my mother, the self-appointed keeper of my shelf-life stamp, says. She points with her fork at a man in the corner of the Steak-Out Restaurant, a dive I've just been hired to redecorate. Making this restaurant look four-star will be hard, but not half as hard as getting through lunch without strangling the woman across the table from me. "*He* would make a good husband."

"Oh, you can tell that from across the room?" I ask, wondering how it is she can forget that when we had trouble getting rid of my last husband, she shot him. "Besides being ten minutes away from death if he actually eats all that steak, he's twenty years too old for me and—shallow woman that I am—twenty pounds too heavy. Besides, I am *so* not looking for another husband here. I'm looking to design a new image for this place, looking for some sense of ambience, some feeling, something I can build a proposal on for them."

My mother studies the man in the corner, tilting her head, the better to gauge his age, I suppose. I think she's grimacing, but with all the Botox and Restylane injected into that face, it's hard to tell. She takes another bite of her steak salad, chews slowly so that I don't miss the fact that the steak is a poor cut and tougher than it should be. "You're concentrating on the wrong kind of proposal," she says finally. "Just look at this place, Teddi. It's a dive. There are hardly any other diners. What does *that* tell you about the food?"

"That they cater to a dinner crowd and it's lunchtime," I tell her.

I don't know what I was thinking bringing her here with me. I suppose I thought it would be better than eating alone. There really are days when my common sense goes on vacation. Clearly, this is one of them. I mean, really, did I not resolve less than three weeks ago that I would not let my mother get to me anymore?

What good are New Year's resolutions, anyway?

Mario approaches the man's table and my mother studies him while they converse. Eventually Mario leaves the table with a huff, after which the diner glances up and meets my mother's gaze. I think she's smiling at him. That or she's got indigestion. They size each other up.

I concentrate on making sketches in my notebook and

try to ignore the fact that my mother is flirting. At nearly seventy, she's developed an unhealthy interest in members of the opposite sex to whom she isn't married.

According to my father, who has broken the TMI rule and given me Too Much Information, she has no interest in sex with him. Better, I suppose, to be clued in on what they aren't doing in the bedroom than have to hear what they might be doing.

"He's not so old," my mother says, noticing that I have barely touched the Chinese chicken salad she warned me not to get. "He's got about as many years on you as you have on your little cop friend."

She does this to make me crazy. I know it, but it works all the same. "Drew Scoones is not my little 'friend.' He's a detective with whom I—"

"Screwed around," my mother says. I must look shocked, because my mother laughs at me and asks if I think she doesn't know the "lingo."

What I thought she didn't know was that Drew and I actually tangled in the sheets. And, since it's possible she's just fishing, I sidestep the issue and tell her that Drew is just a couple of years younger than me and that I don't need reminding. I dig into my salad with renewed vigor, determined to show my mother that Chinese chicken salad in a steak place was not the stupid choice it's proving to be.

After a few more minutes of my picking at the wilted leaves on my plate, the man my mother has me nearly engaged to pays his bill and heads past us toward the back of the restaurant. I watch my mother take in his shoes, his suit and the diamond pinkie ring that seems to be cutting off the circulation in his little finger.

"Such nice hands," she says after the man is out of sight. "Manicured." She and I both stare at my hands. I have two popped acrylics that are being held on at weird angles by bandages. My cuticles are ragged and there's marker decorating my right hand from measuring carelessly when I did a drawing for a customer.

Twenty minutes later she's disappointed that he managed to leave the restaurant without our noticing. He will join the list of the ones I let get away. I will hear about him twenty years from now when—according to my mother—my children will be grown and I will still be single, living pathetically alone with several dogs and cats.

After my ex, that sounds good to me.

The waitress tells us that our meal has been taken care of by the management and, after thanking Mario, the owner, complimenting him on the wonderful meal and assuring him that once I have redecorated his place people will be flocking here in droves (I actually use those words and ignore my mother when she rolls her eyes), my mother and I head for the restroom.

My father—unfortunately not with us today—has the patience of a saint. He got it over the years of living with my mother. She, perhaps as a result, figures he has the patience for both of them, and feels justified having none. For her, no rules apply, and a little thing like a picture of a man on the door to a public restroom is certainly no barrier to using the john. In all fairness, it does seem silly to stand and wait for the ladies' room if no one is using the men's room.

Still, it's the idea that rules don't apply to her, signs don't apply to her, conventions don't apply to her. She knocks on the door to the men's room. When no one answers she gestures to me to go in ahead. I tell her that I can certainly wait for the ladies' room to be free and she shrugs and goes in herself.

Not a minute later there is a bloodcurdling scream from behind the men's room door.

"Mom!" I yell. "Are you all right?"

Mario comes running over, the waitress on his heels. Two customers head our way while my mother continues to scream.

I try the door, but it is locked. I yell for her to open it and she fumbles with the knob. When she finally manages to unlock and open it, she is white behind her two streaks of blush, but she is on her feet and appears shaken but not stirred.

"What happened?" I ask her. So do Mario and the waitress and the few customers who have migrated to the back of the place.

She points toward the bathroom and I go in, thinking it serves her right for using the men's room. But I see nothing amiss.

She gestures toward the stall, and, like any self-respecting and suspicious woman, I poke the door open with one finger, expecting the worst.

What I find is worse than the worst.

The husband my mother picked out for me is sitting on

the toilet. His pants are puddled around his ankles, his hands are hanging at his sides. Pinned to his chest is some sort of Health Department certificate.

Oh, and there is a large, round, bloodless bullet hole between his eyes.

Four Nassau County police officers are securing the area, waiting for the detectives and crime scene personnel to show up. They are trying, though not very hard, to comfort my mother, who in another era would be considered to be suffering from the vapors. Less tactful in the twenty-first century, I'd say she was losing it. That is, if I didn't know her better, know she was milking it for everything it was worth.

My mother loves attention. As it begins to flag, she swoons and claims to feel faint. Despite four No Smoking signs, my mother insists it's all right for her to light up because, after all, she's in shock. Not to mention that signs, as we know, don't apply to her.

When asked not to smoke, she collapses mournfully in a chair and lets her head loll to the side, all without mussing her hair.

Eventually, the detectives show up to find the four patrolmen all circled around her, debating whether to administer CPR, smelling salts or simply call the paramedics. I, however, know just what will snap her to attention.

"Detective Scoones," I say loudly. My mother parts the sea of cops.

"We have to stop meeting like this," he says lightly to

me, but I can feel him checking me over with his eyes, making sure I'm all right while pretending not to care.

"What have you got in those pants?" my mother asks him, coming to her feet and staring at his crotch accusingly. "*Baydar?* Everywhere we Bayers are, you turn up. You don't expect me to buy that this is a coincidence, I hope."

Drew tells my mother that it's nice to see her, too, and asks if it's his fault that her daughter seems to attract disasters.

Charming to be made to feel like the bearer of a plague.

He asks how I am.

"Just peachy," I tell him. "I seem to be making a habit of finding dead bodies, my mother is driving me crazy and the catering hall I booked two freakin' years ago for Dana's bat mitzvah has just been shut down by the Board of Health!"

"Glad to see your luck's finally changing," he says, giving me a quick squeeze around the shoulders before turning his attention to the patrolmen, asking what they've got, whether they've taken any statements, moved anything, all the sort of stuff you see on TV, without any of the drama. That is, if you don't count my mother's threats to faint every few minutes when she senses no one's paying attention to her.

Mario tells his waitstaff to bring everyone espresso, which I decline because I'm wired enough. Drew pulls him aside and a minute later I'm handed a cup of coffee that smells divinely of Kahlúa.

The man knows me well. Too well.

His partner, whom I've met once or twice, says he'll

interview the kitchen staff. Drew asks Mario if he minds if he takes statements from the patrons first and gets to him and the waitstaff afterward.

"No, no," Mario tells him. "Do the patrons first." Drew raises his eyebrow at me like he wants to know if I get the double entendre. I try to look bored.

"What is it with you and murder victims?" he asks me when we sit down at a table in the corner.

I search them out so that I can see you again, I almost say, but I'm afraid it will sound desperate instead of sarcastic.

My mother, lighting up and daring him with a look to tell her not to, reminds him that *she* was the one to find the body.

Drew asks what happened *this time*. My mother tells him how the man in the john was "taken" with me, couldn't take his eyes off me and blatantly flirted with both of us. To his credit, Drew doesn't laugh, but his smirk is undeniable to the trained eye. And I've had my eye trained on him for nearly a year now.

"While he was noticing you," he asks me, "did *you* notice anything about him? Was he waiting for anyone? Watching for anything?"

I tell him that he didn't appear to be waiting or watching. That he made no phone calls, was fairly intent on eating and did, indeed, flirt with my mother. This last bit Drew takes with a grain of salt, which was the way it was intended.

"And he had a short conversation with Mario," I tell him. "I think he might have been unhappy with the food, though he didn't send it back."

Drew asks what makes me think he was dissatisfied, and I tell him that the discussion seemed acrimonious and that Mario looked distressed when he left the table. Drew makes a note and says he'll look into it and asks about anyone else in the restaurant. Did I see anyone who didn't seem to belong, anyone who was watching the victim, anyone looking suspicious?

"Besides my mother?" I ask him, and Mom huffs and blows her cigarette smoke in my direction.

I tell him that there were several deliveries, the kitchen staff going in and out the back door to grab a smoke. He stops me and asks what I was doing checking out the back door of the restaurant.

Proudly—because, while he was off forgetting me, dropping by only once in a while to say hi to Jesse, my son, or drop something by for one of my daughters that he thought they might like, I was getting on with my life— I tell him that I'm decorating the place.

He looks genuinely impressed. "Commercial customers? That's great," he says. Okay, that's what he *ought* to say. What he actually says is "Whatever pays the bills."

"Howard Rosen, the famous restaurant critic, got her the job," my mother says. "You met him—the good-looking, distinguished gentleman with the *real* job, something to be proud of. I guess you've never read his reviews in *Newsday*."

Drew, without missing a beat, tells her that Howard's reviews are on the top of his list, as soon as he learns how to read.

"I only meant—" my mother starts, but both of us assure her that we know just what she meant.

"So," Drew says. "Deliveries?"

I tell him that Mario would know better than I, but that I saw vegetables come in, maybe fish and linens.

"This is the second restaurant job Howard's got her," my mother tells Drew.

"At least she's getting *something* out of the relationship," he says.

"If he were here," my mother says, ignoring the insinuation, "he'd be comforting her instead of interrogating her. He'd be making sure we're both all right after such an ordeal."

"I'm sure he would," Drew agrees, then looks me in the eyes as if he's measuring my tolerance for shock. Quietly he adds, "But then maybe he doesn't know just what strong stuff your daughter's made of."

It's the closest thing to a tender moment I can expect from Drew Scoones. My mother breaks the spell. "She gets that from me," she says.

Both Drew and I take a minute, probably to pray that's all I inherited from her.

"I'm just trying to save you some time and effort," my mother tells him. "My money's on Howard."

Drew withers her with a look and mutters something that sounds suspiciously like "fool's gold." Then he excuses himself to go back to work.

I catch his sleeve and ask if it's all right for us to leave. He says sure, he knows where we live. I say goodbye to Mario. I assure him that I will have some sketches for him in a few days, all the while hoping that this murder doesn't cancel his redecorating plans. I need the money desperately, the alternative being borrowing from my parents and being strangled by the strings.

My mother is strangely quiet all the way to her house. She doesn't tell me what a loser Drew Scoones is—despite his good looks—and how I was obviously drooling over him. She doesn't ask me where Howard is taking me tonight or warn me not to tell my father about what happened because he will worry about us both and no doubt insist we see our respective psychiatrists.

She fidgets nervously, opening and closing her purse over and over again.

"You okay?" I ask her. After all, she's just found a dead man on the toilet, and tough as she is that's got to be upsetting.

When she doesn't answer me I pull over to the side of the road.

"Mom?" She refuses to meet my eyes. "You want me to take you to see Dr. Cohen?"

She looks out the window as if she's just realized we're on Broadway in Woodmere. "Aren't we near Marvin's Jewelers?" she asks, pulling something out of her purse.

"What have you got, Mother?" I ask, prying open her fingers to find the murdered man's ring.

"It was on the sink," she says in answer to my dropped jaw. "I was going to get his name and address and have you return it to him so that he could ask you out. I thought it was a sign that the two of you were meant to be together."

"He's dead, Mom. You understand that, right?" I ask. You never can tell when my mother is fine and when she's in la-la land.

"Well, I didn't know that," she shouts at me. "Not at the time."

I ask why she didn't give it to Drew, realize that she wouldn't give Drew the time in a clock shop and add, "...or one of the other policemen?"

"For heaven's sake," she tells me. "The man is dead, Teddi, and I took his ring. How would that look?"

Before I can tell her it looks just the way it is, she pulls out a cigarette and threatens to light it.

"I mean, really," she says, shaking her head like it's my brains that are loose. "What does he need with it now?"

Silhouette®

nocturne™

**WAS HE HER SAVIOR
OR HER NIGHTMARE?**

HAUNTED
LISA CHILDS

Years ago, Ariel and her sisters were separated for
their own protection. Now the man who vowed
revenge on her family has resumed the hunt, and
Ariel must warn her sisters before it's too late.
The closer she comes to finding them, the more
secretive her fiancé becomes. Can she trust the man
she plans to spend eternity with? Or has he been
waiting for the perfect moment to destroy her?

On sale December 2006.

In February, expect *MORE*
from

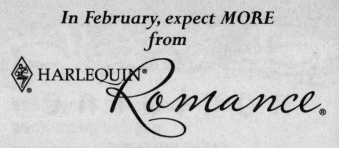

HARLEQUIN® *Romance*®

as it increases to six titles per month.

What's to come…

Rancher and Protector

Part of the
Western Weddings
miniseries

BY JUDY CHRISTENBERRY

---

*The Boss's
Pregnancy Proposal*

BY RAYE MORGAN

Don't miss February's
incredible line up of authors!

www.eHarlequin.com

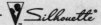
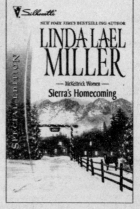

REQUEST YOUR FREE BOOKS!

2 FREE NOVELS PLUS 2 FREE GIFTS!

HARLEQUIN®

INTRIGUE®

Breathtaking Romantic Suspense

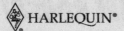